Prophetess

Heroines of the Bible
Book Three

Margy Pezdirtz

Formatting by Daniel J. Mawhinney
www.40DayPublishing.com

Cover design by Jonna Feavel
www.40DayGraphics.com

Printed in the United States of America

To and for my beloved granddaughters:
Desiree
Brittany
Victoria
Amber

And for my special adopted granddaughter,
Caitlin.

"Only take care, and keep your soul diligently, lest you forget the things that your eyes have seen, and lest they depart from your heart all the days of your life. Make them known to your children and your children's children"
—Deuteronomy 4:9

One—the Message

Miriam sat on her couch watching delicate fingers of smoke slowly rising from the fire pit, lazily drifting toward the open sides of the tent like a silent dance through time. Each ember floating upward seemed to carry another of her memories was being offered up as a sacrifice. It wouldn't be long now before The Light arrived to carry her away just as the smoke carried the embers out of the tent. She wondered if she had taught them enough, the ones she was leaving behind. Would they know? Would they remember?

'It was a miracle', she thought as she watched the most recent ember float up and then die out. 'It was all a miracle. Every step. Every action. All of it.' Miriam allowed herself the luxury of drifting back through her life as she sat waiting on her granddaughter, Sarah, to come to the tent. When The Light appeared to her in the night vision and told her of her imminent departure, he instructed her to make sure someone in her family knew the story so it wouldn't be lost in the passing of time.

Sarah, her eldest granddaughter and the one she was the closest to had been her choice to carry forth the telling of their family history. She would be the keeper and protector of the *Aggadah*. It would be her responsibility to carry the story to others so that it can be passed down through the generations. Ari, Miriam's grandson and Sarah's cousin, had gone to summons Sarah to her grandmother's tent.

'Time,' she thought, 'how did it go so quickly? Could we be here already? Can this be the end of my life when there is still so much left undone? It isn't my decision. I have to admit, I've known for some time that The Light would be coming soon. I've expected it. But now that I know I also know how much is being left to the next generation.' She thought about that – the next generation. Were they responsible enough to carry it forward? Would it matter to them? She didn't know but she knew she would have to trust as there was no other way at this point.

Her thoughts drifted back to when she first knew, first understood that she was different, that she was chosen. 'Could I really have been only three? Or maybe it was four. Aaron was a new baby. It was the first time I had actually seen a baby born,' her musings continued. 'Mother, Yochebed, had been a midwife from the time she was a young woman and she wanted me, her daughter, 'my Meri' she called me, to grow up understanding the birthing process. She was determined I was going to grow up and be a midwife, just as she was, so she reasoned that it was important that I not be afraid.' Miriam smiled, remembering that distant conversation and the fear she had held in her heart. 'As usual, *Ema* had her way and instructed the midwife assisting her in the birth to allow me to stay.' She smiled again, this time at the remembrance of the determination and strength of her mother.

The joy of that birth reflected on Miriam's face as she remembered that day, causing a slight wrinkle near her eyes, forming tiny lines in her otherwise beautiful complexion. She had maintained her beauty even in the harshness of almost forty years on the desert. She laughed as she remembered the thrill of knowing that she was now a big sister. She was excited to have a little brother. She loved him so much. He had become her favorite toy and she wanted to hold him, play with him, and most of all, help feed him. More than anything else, she wanted to be with him all the time hating it when she had to do her chores. On the eighth day, the day of his circumcision, her parents gave a party where they announced the name of their baby. He would be called Aaron which meant 'lofty, exalted, high mountain'. She wondered if they'd had any inclination then of just how very important her brother would be to his people, the Hebrews.

The tent flaps parted, breaking into Miriam's pondering of the past. Sarah, smiling at her beloved grandmother, quietly entered the tent. "Good Morning, Softa," she said as she strolled toward her look-alike grandmother, a hug on her mind. "Are you okay? Ari told me you wanted me to come to you right away. That scared me. Are you sick?"

"No, my darling. I'm not sick. In fact, I'm perfectly healthy. Sit down. I have heard from The Light. I have some things to tell you. We need to be able to spend some time together."

Sarah pulled one of the round, heavily embroidered floor cushions over toward her grandmother. She was puzzled over what could be so important that she wanted her to come this early but having a sense of dread over what she might hear. She situated herself next to her grandmother where she, too, could see the fire.

"The Light?" she questioned.

Watching the fire embers had always been one of their shared loves. When she was little they imagined scenes and faces in the fire and they'd laugh. They both loved watching the glowing embers dance, burst forth with light then die out. It was what they had always done when she was a child and it was story time – sit in front of the fire, tell stories and watch the embers. Now she was an adult with children of her own, yet she loved the tradition and had carried it forward with her little ones.

"What is it, Softa? What's on your mind so early in the morning on this beautiful 8th of Nissan?"

Miriam took her hand in hers and rejoiced in the life she felt flowing through the pulse of Sarah's strong hands. "You are a strong woman, Sarah. You are like me and your Abba, you are strong. God has given you strength, not just physical strength, but inner strength as well. I am so proud of you."

Sarah blushed. Confused, once again she asked her grandmother, "Softa, what's happening. I know something is on your heart or you would not have called me to come to you so early this morning. What is it?"

"I saw him. In my dreams – in my night visions - I saw him. He told me it is time and that I was to tell you."

"Wait a minute. You saw who? Who told you to tell me what?" She looked at her grandmother and saw the seriousness of her countenance. "You are scaring me. What are you talking about?"

Miriam reached up and brushed a wisp of Sarah's ever-so-curly jet black hair from her forehead and smiled at her. Her piercing blue eyes were questioning, waiting, looking for an answer. "What?" she whispered, her face etched with concern.

"In my dream, The Light appeared to me. He told me he would be back for me in two days and I needed to make sure that I have told you the story of our people."

"The Light? Oh. No! You can't mean it? It isn't time. You are too young. There is too much to do." Sarah protested, tears welling in her eyes.

"It is time, darling. I've known it for some time now. You know Adonai promised our parents, Moses', Aaron's and mine, your great grandparents, that we would never know the death of ordinary people. It isn't because we are special, but because He used us to bring our people out of captivity. We have never been sick or injured, or anything like that. Adonai promised and He keeps His promises."

"But, no! I don't want you to go. I'm not ready! I need you." Sarah squeezed her grandmother's strong hands. She couldn't let her go. She wouldn't!

"I guess we are never ready for these things, but this isn't the end. You know we believe we'll meet again, in another world, another life, or maybe in Paradise. It doesn't matter. What matters is that we are righteous in our walk with Adonai. I think we have been. I pray we have been. We've tried. I've messed up a couple of times but all-in-all, I think I have done pretty well. At least I've tried."

"So how long do we have?" Sarah could barely choke the words out, wondering how this could be. How was it her beloved *Softa* would leave her here, alone, without her to talk to or tell her what to do. Where would she turn when she was frightened? Who would help her with her own children?

"I think two days. I'm not sure when the count started as he appeared to me in the night vision. If the count started at *erv* today, then we only have a day and a half. If it was sometime in the night, at the time of the dream, then we may have a full two days."

Sarah wept quietly, trying to understand what her grandmother was telling her. "It is all so much to take in. How can this be? Does *Saba* Caleb know?"

"Yes, darling, he knows. He said, 'he too had felt as though something was going to happen, but he had no idea this would be the something after all that we've been through".

They paused for a few minutes, each woman pulling together her emotions. Sarah had never been without her grandmother. How could she manage without her? she wondered. "I know it isn't about me, but why now? Did he tell you anything? Did he say why or how?"

"Sort of. You know it won't be long now before we, our people, are ready to cross over into the Promised Land. I can feel it in my bones and I know it in my spirit. I've seen it in night visions. We've brought you this far. It is time for the next generation to take over. Most of my generation has passed on, just as Adonai said would happen before we would be allowed to cross over. It is your generation and that of your parents that must lead the way now."

"What are you supposed to tell me? Do you know?"

"Yes, I want, or need, to take you back to the beginning, when our people were in Egypt. You have heard stories about it. How hard it was. Not at first but after the new Pharaoh took over, things got really bad. I need to make sure you know all of our history. This is going to be your responsibility now. I've taught the women Torah, from the time I was tiny. Now it will be up to you not only to continue teaching them Torah but to carry forward the telling of our family. Do you understand?"

Sarah nodded 'yes' as she wiped her eyes. She felt like she wanted to get up and run away but she didn't want to miss one second of being with her grandmother. Not one.

"So let's start at the beginning. At the beginning of our family, that is. You already know a great deal of it but now it is important that you really know it. If you have any questions or there is something you don't understand, then ask. It is important that we get this right while we can."

"Okay. I understand. Where do you want to start?"

They gazed at the embers, wishing this day didn't have to happen but knowing that it was significant that they share this time together. Sarah stifled the urge to sob. She was devastated at the thought of her grandmother not being there for her. She had always been.

"Let's go back to Egypt, not literally, but in the telling. I'd like to start with the early days of Aaron. I think that is probably one of my earliest memories that is totally clear."

Sarah nodded, wiping an errant tear. She struggled to keep her emotions and thoughts under control knowing how very serious her grandmother was about this.

"Aaron was only a toddler when the edict from Pharaoh came forward, that our male babies must be killed at birth. No one really understood it or the reasoning behind such a vile thing, but there it was. Delivered with all the pomp and ceremony of a joyous occasion. The couriers read the edict as though it was something to celebrate. Maybe it was to them but not to us.

"It wasn't! It was hideous. It was shocking! Who gave Pharaoh the power to say that from 'This day forward all Hebrew male babies were to be killed!' Why? What had the babies done? They couldn't hurt anyone. They were innocents and that made it even more hideous.

"Why?" was the question as well as the outcry! Why this edict and why at this time? What had happened?

"It didn't take long before we knew. In fact it was within a week that the reason for the edict was revealed. Some of the Hebrew servants working in the *malqata* overheard Pharaoh speaking to one of his generals regarding the reason. Or was it the general reporting to Pharaoh? It wasn't important. What was important was the reason behind it all.

"As it turned out, it was the generals that were afraid of us. In the last census of Goshen, they saw how much the Hebrews had grown in numbers. This concerned them. Ever since the previous final edict that was issued five years before regarding the increase in work expectations from the Hebrews there had been a growing restlessness within our community. Our leader, Amram, my father, your great grandfather, had spoken to Pharaoh representing the Hebrews telling him, "'We understand the requirement that you have placed upon us for building the storage cities. While we may not agree with it, we remain thankful that your country – Egypt – took in our forefathers when there was a famine in Canaan. We appreciate that very much. And we appreciate the fact that your fathers gave us the abundant land of Goshen since we are shepherds. We have been willing to work for you to build the cities, without pay, as you have required, but this is too much! You cannot expect us to stand idly by and allow our male babies to be murdered. How can any parent do that?'"

"Out! Out!" Pharaoh shouted, pointing his golden *wAs*-scepter, with the elongated animal head, toward the long hallway. "You cannot expect me to justify my orders to you! I owe you nothing! You owe me and my country everything! You and your people owe your very lives to us. You should be thankful we aren't killing all of you! Out!"

"I remember that day," Miriam said. "As small as I was at the time, I remember that day. *Abba* came home from the *malqata* and told the leaders of our tribes what had happened. He wept. He literally wept." She paused for a moment, wiping the involuntary tears that flowed from her eyes, down her cheeks as she leaned forward, as though she was reaching into the embers to pull out the hideousness of that vile day.

"When he told my mother, she screamed in agony and collapsed to her knees. She knew she couldn't do it. None of the Hebrew midwives could do it. How could you expect a woman who helps her sisters on the birthing stool to take that newborn baby and kill it? How? It couldn't be done. It wouldn't be done. There had to be a way to escape this edict."

She reached her hand toward Sarah, looking for reassurance in the terrifying memory of that day. Tears poured down her cheeks. She pulled a rag from a basket near her and wiped her face, struggling to continue.

"Pharaoh knew that, too. At least he understood my people enough to know that we would never willing kill one of our own. And a baby? No. That wouldn't happen. So he did what no one had expected him to do. He ordered that the Hebrew midwives could no longer assist in the birthing and he sent in Egyptian midwives to take their place.

"My abba, your *saba raba*, called the leaders of the Tribes together again to discuss what they could do about this. I remember my *ema* crying and pleading with Adonai. It was a hard

13

time. Everyone was sad and worried. But no one expected the Council of the Tribes to come up with the decision they came up with. No one."

"What did they decide?" asked Sarah.

Miriam wiped another trickle from her eyes. "They decided the only thing they could do was to divorce their wives and live apart from them. That was all they could think to do." she answered.

"But, they didn't really do that, did they?"

A slow, soft smile came across Miriam's now tired face. "No. They didn't. They did at first but then they changed their minds."

"How? What changed their minds?"

"I guess you could say Adonai did."

"Really? How did that happen? Did Adonai appear to them?"

"No. He talked to me. You see, by then I was six, going on seven years old. When I was about five I was playing with some other children when I was suddenly lifted from there and pulled towards a bright light. I didn't know what it was but I wasn't afraid."

"What was it?" Sarah asked.

"It was the Spirit of Adonai. The *Rauch HaKodesh*. He pulled me into another room-like area and began showing me things to come. I didn't understand it all but He said that was alright, that He would reveal it to me when the time was right. Then He told me to go back to my parents and give them a message and He was gone."

"A message? What was it? Tell me, Softa."

Miriam thought for a while, not out of forgetfulness but out of the need to revisit the moment. It was the first time she had audibly heard and been instructed by Adonai. Even then she knew it was a moment she would never forget. She wanted to touch that moment again, to linger in the sweet aroma of it, soaking it in as though it were a roadmap to their future.

"Softa? Are you awake?"

"Yes. I'm awake. Adonai gave me a message for the Tribes but I was to deliver it to my *abba* and let him take it to them. I was to stay in the background. That was my assignment."

"What was the message?"

"Yes," she nodded. "The message. The message was that if the men and women, the married couples, stayed away from each other they were pronouncing death to us as a people. They were worse than Pharaoh. He had issued the edict that only the male babies were to die. If the married couples didn't come together, then there wouldn't be any girl babies either and in time our people would die out."

"You did that? You told them that?"

"Yes, I told my *abba*. I didn't have any choice, really. I had entered into The Light, I saw the future with The Light and without The Light. I had to tell my *abba* and he had to take it from there."

"What happened?"

Miriam smiled. "My *abba* questioned me at length. He wanted to know every detail. Every sound. Every smell. Everything. He said he had to be certain that I really had been taken into The Light and this wasn't just a child's fantasy. We talked for a long time. When he was finally satisfied that what I was saying was from Adonai, he called the Council of the Tribes together and told them."

"Were you scared?"

"I don't remember being particularly scared. I do remember a strange feeling in my tummy, more like a warm glow. I'm not sure how to describe it but there was this sense of certainty I guess you would call it. You have to remember, I was only six, almost seven. I don't remember for sure whether it was before my birthday or not. I think it was before though."

"Then what happened? What did they do? Obviously we didn't die out!"

Miriam laughed. "You are so like me. You have to know everything, don't you Sarah?"

"Yes. I want to know. What happened?"

"There was a wedding, that's what happened."

"Who got married?"

"My parents. Your great grandparents."

"But they were already married, weren't they? Wait a minute. Now I'm confused."

"Yes. They had been married. But remember, when Pharaoh issued the edict they separated themselves – like a divorce – from one another and they weren't living together as husband and wife anymore. Now they were going to come back together."

"They were going to come back together because of what you said?"

"Actually, it was because of what Adonai said. You see, He made them realize that what they were doing was against everything we believed. Adonai had told our forefathers, Abraham and Sarah – our patriarchs, to be fruitful and multiply. By living apart, divorcing each other, there wouldn't be any fruit of the marriage. There wouldn't be any babies, male or female, therefore they couldn't multiply. They wouldn't even survive."

"So why the wedding? Why didn't they just move back in together?"

"I guess it was a message being delivered to the entire community. They wanted everyone to know we had received a message from Adonai and that our faith is in Him, not in Pharaoh. By having a public wedding they were making a statement. Life would continue and Adonai would reckon with Pharaoh."

"That took a lot of faith, didn't it?" Sarah asked quietly.

"Yes, but what else did we have. Pharaoh was taking everything from us. We had to move forward and the best way to do it was publicly, out in the open. You could say it was a witness to Pharaoh that we trusted in God, not him."

"That was dangerous, wasn't it?"

"I guess so. But it wasn't as dangerous as letting the entire community die. We had to be obedient to God if we were going to survive. There really wasn't any other choice."

"What happened then?"

"Moses. Moses happened then. It wasn't long before *Ema* announced that she was with child."

"Did you know?"

"Know what?"

16

"Well, you've always been a prophetess. Did you know that she would have a baby and it would be a boy?"

"Yes. I guess I did. I remember feeling responsible for him. I knew my mother would have a child that would become our deliverer. I assumed this would be that child."

"Why?"

"Well, it was because of what I said to my *abba* and what he told the Council that caused all of the husbands and wives to come back together again."

"But it wasn't your fault."

"It wasn't anyone's fault. It was God's directive and that's what I want you to remember, Sarah. It was a miracle. All of it. The whole story from the time of the edict until now is one never-ending miracle. Even these years on the desert. We've experienced one miracle after another."

"How can that be? You said it's time for you to leave? How can that be a miracle?" This time tears came to Sarah's eyes. "I don't want you to leave, Softa. Please don't go."

"But you see, darling, that's part of the miracle. There is a time for everything. At least I'm not sick. He told me it was time but He has given me enough time and warning to tell you the story, again, to make sure you understand. It's too important not to pass down to the generations and that is going to be your responsibility, Sarah, to keep the story alive."

"Are you afraid?"

"No. Not at all. Remember, I told you I saw The Light when I was a child. I saw that same light in him, in the Messenger. I'm not afraid. The Light is welcoming and comforting."

"But Softa, what will I do without you. You've always been here to help me. It will be so lonely now."

"No, Sarah, it won't be lonely. I have the distinct feeling your life will be very full. Don't cry now. We have a lot to do. We need to talk. You need to hear again and remember so you can pass the stories on to your children and their children. We cannot forget. You must not forget."

Two—Pharaoh's Daughter

They quietly watched as another ember floated heavenward. Was it a guiding light or was it just the normal process of a fire and a life dying out?

Sarah broke the silence. "What happened with Moses? You said he came into the world after the wedding. I think that means they got pregnant on their wedding night."

"Yes, that's what happened. It wasn't any time until *Ema* told *Abba*, and then me, that she was with child. It was a time of mixed emotions. We were excited about the baby. We were excited that Adonai's will was being carried out and we were afraid."

"The fear was because the baby might be a boy?"

"Yes, of course. While every Hebrew family wants a lot of children, and especially boys so there will be someone to take care of the parents in their old age, this time a boy baby would be difficult. The edict loomed over all of us. I would hear my parents talking long into the night about what to do if the baby was a boy."

"Could you hear what they were saying?"

"Sometimes a word or two would drift out that would be clear enough to understand. I knew they were considering all kinds of things."

"What were they considering?"

"The biggest question seemed to be whether or not they could escape from Egypt. Could they sneak out by dark and make it across the Nile and on up to the other side of the Yom Suph before being found out by Pharaoh's troops? That was always the question."

"Then why didn't they?"

"Lots of reasons, I suppose. There was the question of whether or not all four of us, soon to be five, could get out. *Ema* refused to go without *Abba*. *Abba* said he couldn't go because he would be missed too soon and they would come looking for us. He said we would have a better chance of making it to the Nile without him. He would join us later, when they were no longer suspicious. He wanted *Ema* to take me and *Dohd* Aaron and go but she refused. She said all or none."

"You were little then. What did you want to happen?"

"I just wanted it all to stop. It was so frightening. I was afraid Pharaoh and his troops would ride their horses into our house at night and kill all of us. I had a lot of bad dreams."

"Was there any chance of that really happening?"

"To a little kid around six or seven years old? Yes it was a huge chance. Today, probably not."

Miriam smiled. "Nothing happened for a while. Life went on pretty much as it always had. *Ema* was still a midwife and she would try to beat the Egyptian midwives to the birthing stool. Sometimes she did. Sometimes she didn't. I do remember her telling us a story though about how they – the midwives – would question her and the other Hebrew midwives. They always wanted to know why it was that the Hebrew women had their babies so quickly and easily."

"What do you mean quickly and easily?"

"The Egyptian midwives were the only ones that were supposed to deliver the babies but by the time they got to the area where the birthing process had been going on, the babies were already born and taking in nourishment if they were girls. If they were boys, someone would take them and run with them. Sometimes they got away. Sometimes they didn't. We never knew for sure as it was all hush, hush since it was a life or death matter."

"What did the Egyptian midwives do then?"

"If they got there in time, they would do what Pharaoh told them to do. They would take the newborn baby boys and throw them in the Nile saying they were offering them up to *Nile Iterw*, the god of the Nile"

"How horrible." tears trickled from Sarah's eyes. "Just the thought of it …it's just too much."

"Yes, it was. It was very sad. But Adonai intervened."

"How?"

"The Egyptian midwives were touched by the fact that the women were willing to sacrifice their own lives rather than the lives of their boy babies. A lot of different stories surfaced but we never knew for sure what was true and what was fantasy. However, eventually the midwives began understanding our God and they, also, began trying to hide the babies."

"How did Pharaoh handle that?"

"Like he handled everything. He threw tantrums, made threats, promised retaliation, so forth. That didn't stop it though."

"Do you really think he had issued the edict because of the number of Hebrews or was something else involved?"

"We all came to think it was because of his prophets. Somehow they learned that a Hebrew savior would be born and he would lead us out of Egypt to freedom. That meant we would be led out of captivity back to our homeland, to Canaan. They told Pharaoh. I think that was what he was afraid of more than anything else. He was a bully. He needed someone to pick on and the Hebrews were easy as we were still considered 'guests' in his land although he had forced us into hard labor. Guests wasn't exactly a term that fit our people any more. If we left he wouldn't have slave labor then what would he do? Who would build his storage cities?"

"What happened to the Egyptian midwives? Did they get into trouble with Pharaoh?"

"A little at first. They got by with it though when they told him that we were such strong women that we pushed the babies out faster than they could get there."

"Was that true?"

"Maybe. At first. But they saw truth. They saw that the edict to kill the babies was hideous and against God, not only ours but some of their gods as well. They refused to do it so the only thing they could do was tell Pharaoh a lie. Adonai rewarded them though by promising them their names would be remembered throughout history. Who knows, maybe someday we'll name our

Hebrew daughters for the midwives of Egypt. Can you imagine one of your great granddaughters being named Puah? Or maybe Shiprah?"

They both laughed. It was a new idea, a strange thought for them but they knew that the day would come when that likely would happen. Sarah mused to herself what it would be like to have a grandchild, or a great grandchild called by an Egyptian name. She'd have to think about that one. It would be an adjustment, but then wasn't everything these days.

"So what happened when Moses was born?"

"Ah, Moses. How I loved that baby. It was scary for all of us. The Light had spoken to me again, before my parents wedding, and told me that my mother would bear a child that would deliver us from captivity. I told my parents. At first they were shocked, then excited, then humbled. We all knew that a deliverer for us would have to be a man in order to fit all of the prophecies. That meant the deliverer would be a boy baby and his life would be in constant danger. It was very scary."

"What happened? What did you do? What did my great grandparents do?"

"Lots of things. *Ema* tried to hide her pregnancy. She did that pretty well for a while, but as with all pregnant women, her belly grew until she could no longer hide it. She stayed in the house a great deal going with the idea that the less people that knew about the coming child the better. I heard her crying. I heard her pleading with Adonai. A couple of times I even heard my parents arguing about what they should do. There didn't seem to be a good answer."

"How did she hide her pregnancy? How did they manage to hide him for so long?"

"It wasn't easy. He was born in the middle of the night. *Ema's* labor wasn't very long. It was another miracle, a miracle bigger than having a baby. It was like Adonai's hand of protection was on the baby and *Ema* from the very beginning. And he didn't cry."

"How can that be? I've never heard of a baby not crying?"

"That's right. As long as he was in our home surrounded by the family, he didn't cry. It was almost like he was a silent

22

baby. A time or two my parents talked about it. They already had two older children so they knew babies cried, a lot! In fact, they wondered if something was wrong with Moses because he didn't cry. There was no doubt he was a special child but we didn't understand all of it. We prayed."

"Whose idea was it to put him in the basket?"

"*Ema's*. I heard that conversation. In fact, they told me to come and listen. The idea was that they could no longer hide him. He was getting bigger and he was getting stronger. They prayed a lot, then they, actually, *Ema* decided, that if Pharaoh ordered that the Hebrew babies be put in the Nile, she would put her baby in the Nile and trust Adonai to take care of him."

"That is amazing. I cannot imagine what she must have gone through."

"No. I'm sure none of us understood her emotions nor her trust. She sent me to get the tar and pitch from the merchants. She thought they wouldn't ask me as many questions as they would her. Even that was a gamble. But I got them for her and ran back to the house with them. At that time, I didn't know what the tar and pitch was for just in case someone asked a lot of questions."

"Were you scared?"

"No, not really. I was young and I'm not sure I understood everything at that point. When I got back to the house with the tar and pitch – the clay - I helped her coat the basket. We put the tar on the outside and the clay on the inside so it would block the harsh smell of the tar from the baby. She wanted to make sure it could hold the baby and stay afloat. She put several layers of the tar on it then waited for them to dry."

"I wonder what she was thinking."

"I don't know. I saw her wipe tears several times but she never said anything. She made a special blanket to wrap him in. Then when the basket was dry and she was sure it wouldn't sink, we wrapped him in the special blanket and gently placed the basket, baby and all, in the Nile. We prayed. Oh did we ever pray." She paused, reflecting on the emotions of putting her baby brother in the water, not knowing what to expect. "That was so hard to put that little doll into the water but we didn't have a lot of choice"

Both women sat in silence for a short while thinking about the terror Yochebed must have felt when she placed that little guy in the water.

"I looked up at her and asked her if she wanted me to follow the basket. The current was beginning to carry it away from where we were. She didn't try to hide the tears when she looked at me and said, 'Yes, I need to know what happens. But please be careful. I can't lose both of you.'"

"How far did it go?"

"That's another one of the many miracles. It didn't go all that far, maybe a mile or so. It was morning and Pharaoh's daughter, Princess *Bithiah*, and her handmaidens were at the Nile. They had come down in the early morning hours, before it got too hot, to bathe. Rumors were that the Princess was ill so bathing in the Nile was a healing act for her. By now, the baby was crying in the basket. I think that was the first time I ever heard him cry."

"Really?"

"Yes, come to think of it. It was the first and only time I heard him cry. I guess Adonai had kept him silent to protect him and now he was crying to protect him. It was the cry that caused the Princess to look up and see the basket floating toward her."

"What happened?"

"You know what happened," Miriam smiled, "I've told you this before. But I love telling it anyway. The crying alerted the Princess to the baby. She sent one of her handmaidens that could swim, out to get the basket. I think she knew immediately what it was. Anyway, the handmaiden pulled the basket to the bank where the Princess was. Another handmaiden pulled the blanket off of him and the Princess bent down and picked him up."

"I watched as they removed the blanket from him then his diaper. There was no question he was a Hebrew baby boy. He was circumcised and marked with the Covenant of God."

"Were you afraid?"

"Oddly enough, no. I felt like the hand of God was pushing me forth. I walked right into that crowd of women and said, 'Would you like for me to get one of the Hebrew women to nurse the child?' It was a boldness that I had never experienced before."

"How old were you?

"Mmmm, probably eight. It doesn't matter. At that point I was ageless. It wasn't about me anymore, it was about God, the Hebrews, the baby, the Princess. Everything just swirled around into one big event. It was amazing. Then the other miracle happened."

"What was that?"

"The Princess said, 'Yes!' Do you understand what an amazing miracle that was? Here was an illegal Hebrew child plucked out of the water by the daughter of the very man that had demanded that he be thrown into the water. That was a miracle. Then when she sent me to get a nursemaid for the child, surely she knew or at least had to think about the fact that I would get his own mother to do the job. Then on top of that, the Princess gave the baby back to his own mother."

"Why would she do that?

"God! Who else could have orchestrated such an event? Not only did *Ema* get her baby back to have and hold until he was weaned, which would have been at three, but she was going to get paid for taking care of her own child. Sometimes I have to shake my head and wonder at the awesomeness of Adonai. He is fascinating."

"What do you think Pharaoh said about it all?"

"I imagine he knew then that he had lost a long battle. Everyone knew he was crazy over his daughter, Princess *Bithiah*, and he would give her anything she wanted. No one would ever have thought he would allow her to have, and raise as her own, the very savior of the Hebrew people that he tried to wipe out. God's sense of humor is delightful.

"You know his name, Moses, means 'plucked from the water'. Here he is being raised in the palace by Pharaoh's daughter and every time he calls him by his name it has to be a reminder to him that this is the child he tried to kill. Do you see the pattern of miracles here?"

"Yes, Softa, I see them. It truly is a delightful story. What happened then?"

"Things quieted down a lot. All of a sudden babies were no longer being thrown into the water. Families grew. Life continued. But so did the persecution. It was almost like Egypt was angry and for no reason. The Egyptian taskmasters began to push for more and more, like they wanted to kill our people but didn't have permission so they'd work us to death. It didn't happen though.

"The entire slavery thing started because of the hatred the Egyptians had developed toward us. We never understood why or what caused the hatred. Initially, they placed a 'tax' on our heads. We had to pay Egypt so much money per member of our family for the privilege of living in Egypt. We didn't have money. We were shepherds. We had animals and lots of people, but no money. Then they said we could 'work it off' by working for them for free. But the bill was never considered paid. They said we didn't work hard enough or long enough or seriously enough. We couldn't get ahead. The pressure continued. They pushed harder and harder, trying to wipe us out but it didn't happen. We continued to grow. The more they pushed the more growth we experienced. It was like living in a press of some kind but we felt that God was with us even though we couldn't see Him."

"How long did this happen?"

"Years." Miriam paused, a look of deep sorrow came over her face as she reflected back over those days. "Our people cried out to God. We needed help. We needed the promised savior. We begged for him. Nothing happened. Life continued. The pressure continued."

Three—Moses

"I grew up, met your *Saba* Caleb and got married. That was another miracle, my own personal miracle. I was of the Tribe of Levi. *Saba* Caleb is of the Tribe of Judah. We were different by patriarchal families but we were one and the same in spirit. Our families were different although we were all related. My mother, Yochebed – your great grandmother – was born to Levi, a son of Jacob, the day Jacob and his sons arrived in Egypt. They didn't even make it to Goshen before she was born. Technically, she was an Egyptian by birth, but we were all Hebrews although we didn't really use that term then.

"Your *Saba Raba* Amram was also of the tribe of Levi and was her nephew. His father was Kohath, one of the sons of Levi. Even so, he was older than my *ema* by a year. They had probably known each other as children but as time passed and the situation in Egypt became harsher, people got separated according to the work as well as working such long days. It didn't leave much time for socializing. "

"How did you meet Saba?" Sarah asked, already knowing the story. Still she never tired of hearing it.

"We were just kids, 17 and 18. He was being pushed into forced labor and I was serving as a midwife, just like my mother wanted. One of the women of the Tribe of Judah was having trouble delivering a baby and they had sent for us. *Ema* was delivering another baby so I was rushing there as fast as I could go, concerned about the birthing mother and not paying any attention to where I was walking. I rounded a corner and ran right into your Saba! Somehow I tripped and fell. He leaned over, helped me get up and I looked into his eyes. That's it. I was smitten. He was beautiful."

"What happened to the mother delivering the baby? Did you help her?"

"No, I didn't make it there. I had injured my ankle when I fell and was limping. I told him I needed to get to her but he seemed to know that the midwife was already there. He told me not to worry about it, asked which house was mine, then he carried me home. The rest is history. Our parents met and arranged for us to marry and we've been together ever since.

"That's our personal story but I need to get back to the story of Moses. We knew about Moses but once he moved to the *malqata* we didn't see him anymore unless he was riding through the building projects in his fancy chariot."

"Did he know who you were?"

"I don't know. It didn't seem like it but maybe he did. Once he was weaned and back in the palace of Pharaoh, when he was a little boy, we weren't allowed to see him anymore. "

"How did that make you feel?"

"Confused would be the best word for it. He had been with us until he was three. *Ema* nursed him and taught him. Up to that point he was raised as a Hebrew and all of the teachings that we knew at that time were taught to him. But, he was only a baby – only three. Then he was gone. How much does a three year old child remember about his family when he is no longer with them?

"We didn't see him until he was being taught architecture then he'd show up at some of the building projects. We knew him but I don't think he really knew us."

"What was it like for you when you did see him?"

Miriam smiled, remembering those rare moments. "He was beautiful. He had grown into manhood. His body was well shaped. His hair was always perfectly braided. They couldn't let it just lay naturally as it was too curly where that of the Egyptians was straight. Braiding it seemed to be the only way they could control it. His clothes were regal. He wore a lot of white linen with brilliant golden trim, obviously royal clothing that set him apart. I would step into a doorway or in the shadows to watch him for as long as I possibly could then I'd move on before the guards saw me staring. I couldn't help myself."

"That must have been hard."

"Sometimes it was very hard. I had to fight to control my anger. I wanted to yell at him and ask him if he knew what his people were dealing with. I wanted to ask him if he knew his father had died from the hard labor. But I didn't. I just watched and I waited. I couldn't understand what it was that Adonai was doing and why it was taking so long."

"What do you mean? What were you expecting? How long did you wait?"

"You know the answer to that. We waited for generations. People died. More babies were born. Taskmasters changed but the work didn't. Every day, all day long, no matter the weather or our health or our family situations we had to show up and do our jobs. It was a requirement. If we didn't sign in with the taskmasters our entire family would be sought out and punished. No one dared to be absent unless they were dying then it had better be real."

"I'm sorry, Softa. I didn't know you had it so hard. I guess I did know but it's so easy to forget."

"No. You mustn't forget. Never forget. Tell this story to your children and their children and their children. Tell it again and again until your days are done and it is time for you to leave. Then you can quit telling it. But not until that day."

"I understand. Why isn't this written? Telling the story over and over lends itself to being distorted or forgotten, doesn't it? If we could write it down, it would help a great deal."

"Someday someone will do that. If you want to do it, then now is the time to start. But you must remember what I'm telling you today as I'll be gone tomorrow or the day after."

The words sank deeply into Sarah's heart piercing her thoughts. There was no question in her mind what her grandmother was telling her. She was leaving. How could that be? Everything she had told her in the past came to fruition. She knew this would as well, no matter what either of them wanted.

"I will write it but I'm hearing it and learning it too. You told me a great deal of this when I was a child but now that I have children and my life is so busy I haven't had time to focus on it. I'll try to do better now."

"You'll have to do better than try, my darling. You must do it. This isn't just my story. It's the history of our people, of our family, of you. No scribe can write it all down so I'm telling you now, one last time before I leave. You have to hear it and remember it. Do you understand?"

"Yes. I understand. I don't like it but I understand what you are saying. I will write it and I will keep it. My children and my grandchildren will learn the story and they will tell it to their children. I promise."

"Let's continue then. There is much I have to say and so little time to say it in."

An ember caught in the soft breeze and followed the smoke to the tent opening. Was it an omen? Were these embers keepers of a life now ending?

"Moses was famous for his compassion. Most of Pharaoh's family were cold and stiff, but the well-spoken rumor was that about Moses' great compassion for his people – us – the Hebrews. That was proven one day when he came upon one of the taskmasters beating a Hebrew.

"The taskmaster was especially cruel. He thought nothing of destroying families and marriages. The Hebrew man that was being beaten was the husband of Shelomis, daughter of Divri. The Egyptian taskmaster had gone into their home one morning, awakened the husband and sent him out to work earlier than usual, then he forced himself on Shelomis. When the husband found out about it he wanted to kill the Egyptian for his cruelty but he was too weak and too broken from the work he was assigned to stand up to the strong Egyptian. It was then, when he was confronting the taskmaster, that Moses rode up.

"Moses lost it. He completely lost it. He had heard the story of what the taskmaster had done to Shelomis and he was furious over it. When he saw the fight he became so angry that he jumped out of his chariot, walked up to the taskmaster and slugged him. When he fell he hit his head on a rock and it killed him. Moses dug a pit and hid him in the sand but people knew. There were eyes everywhere. Secrets didn't exist. It was an accident but Pharaoh acted as though it were planned.

"The next day Moses came back to where the men were working. I don't know, maybe he was going to tell them who he was. Maybe he just wanted to talk. We never knew why he came back so soon or what was on his mind. Then he was gone. Just gone."

"Why did he leave? Do you know?"

"I didn't find out until after he came back. It was forty years later before I saw him again."

"Forty years. What was that like? Did you know him?"

"Yes. Yes, I did know him. He had changed a lot. He was dressed in desert clothes. He was dark and wrinkled from the harsh sun. But I knew him. He looked like Abba. Just like him. And Aaron was with him."

"What did he say when he saw you?"

"He didn't remember me at first. Aaron introduced us and he looked at me rather blankly. Then I saw a tiny glimmer of recognition come over him. He nodded his head then Aaron led him away, to the Council to talk to them."

"What were you thinking? How did that feel?"

"I don't know. Expected, I think. You see, I always knew he would come back. He was the anointed one that would lead us out of Egypt. Sometimes in my night visions I would see him coming toward us with a huge staff in his hand, motioning for us to come. Then I would wake up."

"Were you scared?"

"No. Not at all. There was a confidence within me that was hard to describe. I knew. I just knew. I knew my mother had given birth to the savior and Moses was the last child. Aaron was not that kind of leader so it had to be Moses that I was seeing in the night visions. No. I wasn't afraid. I was expecting him."

Four—Plagues

"What happened when he came back? Did he immediately go to Pharaoh with the demands?" Sarah asked.

"No. His wife, Zipporah, and the boys were with him. Gershom and Eliezer. They were all tired from the long journey from Midian. He needed to get them settled in.

"We were so excited to see them, to get to meet his wife and sons. It was like having a long lost family come home. I wanted them to stay with me but they moved in with our mother. She was older and not in good health. Zipporah was wonderful with her, very caring and tender. She was such a good help. She just took over as though she had been here for years and we loved her."

"I remember her."

"Good. Don't ever forget her. I loved her. In fact, that's what got me in trouble but we'll come to that part of the story later. I want to keep things flowing as best as possible so I don't forget anything. And we have to hurry."

"I won't forget her. I remember her deep, dark eyes. When she was angry they were as black and shiny as the tar pits we've passed along the way. And her dark skin was fabulously flawless. She was beautiful. I want to name a daughter for her." Sarah paused, smiling to herself at that thought. "Yes, you are right. Let's go on."

Miriam looked at her granddaughter with eyes of affection and a heart full of thankfulness. She never failed to understand just how much like her Sarah was. She was smart, quick to catch on, thoughtful and energetic. She didn't have the gift of prophecy but she seemed to have extreme wisdom and that was such a blessing to the entire family. She truly was wise beyond her years and it would serve her well.

"Ah, let's see. Where were we? Oh yes. Moses came back. He went to meet with the council of the Tribes but they weren't too happy to see him. That night the story was told of why he left Egypt. It turns out that the day he left he had come up on two of our people, Hebrew men, fighting and he tried to break it up. They challenged him and asked if he was 'going to kill them too?' With that he knew he didn't have any place to hide. Even he had no secrets.

"We hadn't known Pharaoh was furious with him and threatening him over the death of the Egyptian taskmaster. They had a terrible argument over the dead Egyptian then the two Hebrews challenged him and he just panicked and ran. He thought he was running for his life. He said he didn't let down his guard until he got to Midian. He was exhausted from his journey and sat down by a well to rest when he met Zipporah. Much like the story of Jacob, he was sitting there when she and her sisters came with their flocks. They were drawing water to fill the troughs for their sheep when the other shepherds came and tried to frighten them away. Moses rose to the defense of the women and scattered the shepherds. When Zipporah told her father what had happened he offered hospitality to Moses. He told us he felt he was far enough away that no one would find him and he could relax. He willingly traded the scepter of Egypt for a staff of a shepherd and he went about making a new life for himself."

"What a change. It must have been hard for him."

"It was hard for all of us. None of us really knew what had happened. We felt we had lost the only hope we had in the Egyptian hierarchy and there was nothing we could do about it. Pharaoh's henchmen were ready to kill any Hebrew for any reason, including asking questions. We could only keep our heads down and hands stretched heaven ward crying out to God. We begged Him to send a deliverer. In my spirit, in my prophetic spirit, I knew Moses wasn't dead. I wasn't sure where he was, but I knew he was alive. I had seen him in the night vision but the location was sketchy, at best.

"Finally, one day Aaron disappeared. At first we didn't know where he went. He just wasn't here one day. After he had been gone for a while his wife, *Dohdah* Elisheba, told us what had happened. He felt there had been enough death and destruction to our people. He took a shepherd's staff and walked out to the fields with the shepherds. In an earlier conversation I had told him I had seen Moses in the night visions and that he was northeast of where we were, near mountains. Aaron decided to go find him and bring him back. If the prophecy The Light had given me was true, then Moses was to be the deliverer and we needed him, desperately."

"Why hadn't he told you about it? About his leaving?"

"Aaron has always been funny about things like that. He hears God on his own and then he goes and does. Sometimes he tells us, sometimes he doesn't. He has always believed that God had a use for him but he never thought it would be something as important as being the High Priest. But I don't think any of us gave any thought to how much God would use our family, all three of us."

"How long was he gone?"

"Aaron? About three weeks, I think. I'm not sure. We were all busy helping *Dohdah* Elisheba with the boys. Four boys can be a handful and those four were very active. They were always in a hurry. Maybe that's why Nadab and Abihu got into so much trouble with God and He killed them. It was very hurtful."

"So what did the Council say?"

"Like I told you, at first they didn't believe him nor trust him. He told them about everything that had happened, why he had left and where he had been the last forty years. They listened. They weren't too impressed until he told them about the burning bush."

"Oh yes. I forgot that. Please tell me that story again."

"Sarah. You can't forget. Everything depends on your remembering our story. Take notes.

"Moses was working as a shepherd for his father-in-law. One of the sheep, or goats, I'm not sure which, had gone astray and he was out looking for it. He was perfectly happy being a shepherd. Egypt was a long way from his thoughts and so were we and so was our God. He said he saw something brilliant in color and glowing. It looked like a fire but there was no reason for a fire and there wasn't any smoke. He walked closer and saw that it was a bush that looked like it was on fire with flames going forth but the bush wasn't being consumed. He was drawn toward the bush like a magnet. Then he saw the angel, in the bush, and He spoke to him."

"Moses spoke to the angel?"

"No." Miriam laughed. "The angel called out to Moses, speaking to him in a heavenly tongue, but for some miraculous reason, Moses understood him. The angel told him to come near and to remove his sandals because he was standing on holy ground.

"Moses said he was too shocked not to do it or to even question the instructions. He removed his sandals and actually fell on his face before the angel. The angel told him to get up and to listen. He said, 'I am the God of your father, the God of Abraham, the God of Isaac and the God of Jacob'.

"He went on to say he was actually terrified and hid his face again. But the Lord said, 'I have seen the affliction of My people who are in Egypt, and have heard their cry because of their taskmasters. I am aware of their sufferings. I have come down to deliver them from the power of the Egyptians and to bring them up from that land to a good and spacious land, to a land flowing with milk and honey, to the place of the Canaanite, the Hittites, the Amorites, the Perizzites, the Hivites, and the Jebusites. Now listen, the cry of the sons of Israel has come to Me and I have seen the oppression with which the Egyptians are oppressing them.'"

"Oh my goodness, that must have been frightening. What did Moses do?"

"He argued with Him."

"Argued with God? Moses argued with God! That's a little dangerous, isn't it?"

"Yes. For most people. But Moses isn't most people. God was not only calling him back to His people, He was calling him to Himself. Moses actually became God's friend. You know that. What happened then was almost unbelievable unless you believe in miracles. They had a conversation. Adonai started telling Moses what He wanted him to do. He told him that he, Moses, was the chosen one to bring our people out of Egypt.

"Moses argued with Him, saying he wasn't anything or anyone. In fact, they argued for several days there on that hillside, with Moses putting up all the reasons as to why he couldn't do it. He had no power, no authority. He asked, 'Who am I?' He even said, 'You want me to go to Egypt, to Pharaoh who hates me now, that I should bring the sons of Israel out of Egypt?'

"God said, 'Yes! I will be with you. I will prove this to you by giving you a sign. You will bring the people – My people – out of Egypt and back here, to this mountain, to worship me.' Moses, always the stubborn one, said, 'Oh yeah, that's right. I'm going to go to the sons of Israel and I'm going to say to them, 'The God of your fathers has sent me to you.' Then they are going to look at me and say, 'Oh yeah. Prove it. What's His name?' And I don't know the answer to that."

Miriam smiled, remembering the story as Moses told it to them. "'God said to Moses, 'I AM WHO I AM', and He said, 'That is what you are going to say to the Sons of Israel. The Lord, the God of your fathers, the God of Abraham, the God of Isaac and the God of Jacob, has sent me to you.'

"It was quite an encounter. But then, it had to be to get Moses off the back side of the desert and willing to walk in the calling God had placed on his life. It wasn't going to be easy. Then God said, 'You will tell the sons of Israel, *Ehyeh Asher Ehyeh*, I WILL BE WHAT I WILL BE. I am the Lord, the God of your fathers, the God of Abraham, the God of Isaac and the God of Jacob. This is My name forever, and this is My memorial-name to all generations.'

"He didn't leave any room for doubt, which was good. Then He instructed Moses to 'Go and gather the elders of Israel together and say to them, 'The Lord, the God of your fathers, the God of Abraham, Isaac and Jacob, has appeared to me, saying, 'I am very concerned about you and what has been done to you in Egypt. I said I will bring you up out of the affliction in Egypt to the land of the Canaanite, the Hittite, the Amorite, the Perizzite, the Hivite and the Jebusite to a land flowing with milk and honey.'

"God promised Moses that once they understood, the Elders of the Tribes would come together with him and they would go together to the king of Egypt, to Pharaoh, and you will say to him, 'The LORD, the God of the Hebrews, has met with us. So now, please, let us go a three days' journey into the wilderness, that we may sacrifice to the LORD our God.'

"He also told Moses that He knew the king, Pharaoh, wouldn't comply. This was only the beginning. They needed to start with the request, then the warning. It had to be fair. Even so, God knew the king would be obstinate and not allow it. The warning would be that you, Moses, 'will stretch out your hand and strike Egypt with all My miracles. When the king has finally experienced all of My miracles, which will cost him the life of his first born son, he'll let you go. But it will get very hard before that happens. When you do leave Egypt, it won't be empty-handed. Every woman will ask her neighbor for clothing, for articles of silver and gold, and your sons and daughters will go out dressed in dignity instead of slaves clothing. You will plunder the Egyptians just as they have plundered you these many years.'"

"What did you think when you heard this story? Were you frightened? What did you think of Moses? Did you believe him?"

"Yes. I believed him. Remember the prophecy before he was born and the night visions of his beckoning us to follow him. I knew he was going to be the redeemer for us. I had to believe him. But the story doesn't end there."

"Moses said he argued with God?" Sarah mused. "Still?"

"Yes. I told you, he has always been stubborn. He asked God what would happen if the people didn't believe him. Or worse yet, what if Pharaoh didn't believe him. God said, "What is that you are holding in your hand?" Moses thought that was a funny question but he answered, "My staff." Then God told him, "Throw it on the ground." He did and it became a snake. Moses was frightened and jumped away from it. But God told him to pick it up by the tail. He did and it became a staff again."

"What a sight that must have been."

"Yes, I'm sure it was. But you see, God was having to convince Moses that he could do this. Moses knew God could do it but he was having trouble seeing himself in the situation and understanding just what his role was to be. It's easy to understand now, these many years later, but in the moment it wasn't that easy.

"God knew he still didn't believe enough so He told him to put his hand in the cloak over his bosom. Moses did that then pulled it back out. As it came out it turned white, like snow with tzara'at."

Miriam paused, remembering that experience in her own life. She shuttered. It was terrifying then just as the telling of this story was a frightening reminder of what had happened to her. "It didn't last though. God had him put his hand back in and pull it back out. This time it was clear. He went on then to tell Moses of some of the miracles that would happen, beginning with the staff becoming a snake and swallowing their snakes, the Nile turning to blood and so on. God knew exactly what would happen and he told Moses everything.

"He wanted Moses to trust in Him. It wasn't easy for him to do. He had become very self-sufficient at being a shepherd and had come to respect that life style. Moses continued to argue. He said he no longer remembered the Egyptian language. He said he had spent the last forty years speaking another language and hadn't even heard Egyptian for that period of time. On top of that, he no longer remembered the Hebrew language either. He argued that he wouldn't be clear in his speech, that he would stumble and forget words. He didn't think he could do it. God was getting mad now and told him 'not to worry, He was sending Aaron, his big brother, to help him out'. Sure enough that's what happened."

"Did *Dohd* Aaron show up right then?"

"No. But he was on his way. It would be a day or two before they met each other. God continued with the instructions to Moses and told him that he was to be the instructor of Aaron. Aaron would help him but God was only going to talk to Moses and he, in turn, would relay the instructions to Aaron. It seemed like God was setting up a form of government or something. We weren't really sure. We were all very struck at what he told us and how it was supposed to play out. Not everyone was in agreement with it but Moses said they would come around. And, they did – eventually, at least most of them. As you know, these many years later, some still question his authority and capability to lead us."

Five—Freedom

The telling was gently interrupted by Sarah's grandfather, *Saba* Caleb, as he led Miriam's two closest friends, Yael and Irit, into the tent. Each carried a bountiful tray of delicious offerings of manna, prepared in the way that had become their particular specialty. It was obvious they had heard of Miriam's soon departure and they were saddened by it. Having been instructed by Caleb not to disturb the two women, they were struggling, trying to keep their deep emotions under control when they saw her.

Miriam smiled and nodded her thanks to them as they slipped out of the tent, just as quietly as they had entered. She wished she had time to properly thank each of them, to hug them and to reassure them. But there wasn't time.

Grandmother and granddaughter paused for a few minutes to enjoy the delicacies served to them. Aware of the shortness of time Miriam insisted they return to the story, to the telling, while they ate. She didn't want to leave anything out as the history was important.

"Now, where were we? Oh yes. Moses went back to his father-in-law's home, Jethro who was a Midianite priest, and told him what had happened. When Moses first settled in Midian and married Zipporah he promised Jethro he would never leave without his permission. They talked about it that night over dinner around an open fire. Jethro asked a lot of questions and listened carefully to all that Moses told him. They agreed that it was not going to be easy and could even be dangerous. Moses said he knew that but he also knew he had heard from God and that he had to answer the call. He asked his father-in-law for permission to leave and it was granted."

"The next day Moses loaded Zipporah and the two boys, they were small then, on a donkey and started the journey back to Egypt. I am sure he was wrestling with himself over the conversation with Adonai and the instructions he had been given. The journey was long and hard on the children. After two days they finally came to a lodge along the way and arranged to spend the night there so they could all rest.

"It was there that things really turned bad. The Lord sent an angel to attack Moses. As they were wrestling it was revealed that God was upset that he, Moses, had dared to set off on such an important journey without his two sons being circumcised. Zipporah got mad, really mad. She had left behind her family to follow her husband and his God, the same God that caused all of this. Now that same God was trying to kill him! She took a sharpened flint and circumcised the boys herself, threw the foreskins at Moses, called him a name and stomped off with the crying, wounded children in tow. That stopped the attack on Moses and all settled down after that, at least for a while.

"It was apparently at that time that God told Aaron where they were and he went to the lodge and found them. The brothers were delighted to see each other and spent a lot of time talking, catching up and filling in the blanks. They hadn't known each other as brothers until then although they each knew the other existed. I think that was when Zipporah began to see the vastness of the mission that Moses had been called to. It probably scared her. Who wouldn't be scared? It was all so different. Moses was going home. She left home. It was a journey the two of them were going to have to walk together and there was no experience for it."

"It's amazing that she didn't just turn around and go back to her father."

"Yes. But she really loved him. Always did. She wanted to be with him. She just didn't know what was expected of her. And, she didn't think we would accept her since she was a Midianite woman. We did though. She and I became very close."

"So is that when the Council came around and started trusting Moses?"

"Yes. Somewhat. They heard the story of the burning bush and the encounter with the angel. Then they heard how Aaron had found Moses by following the instructions of the Lord. No one could deny that there was a divine plan in place. It was just that no one really knew what was going to happen even though Moses laid it all out for them. Everyone was frightened of the unknown. That is always the hardest part, the unknown."

"They knew in advance about what Pharaoh would do?"

"Yes, they did. Moses had to tell them because everything was going to get so crazy. It took them quite a while to fully agree. Then, after the taskmasters increased the work load they were angry at Moses and wanted him to stop the demands and just leave things be. That was terrible. More work. Less supplies. More demands. More anger. Everything was spinning out of control but Moses held steady and he encouraged us to do the same. Every plague was a direct attack on one of Egypt's god-like idols and the Egyptians were not nice about it."

"How did he manage to keep everything under control? I know, I remember hearing, stories about how angry everyone was and that they blamed him for the increased work load. What happened that he got them to quiet down?"

Miriam chuckled. "I don't think you can say they have ever quieted down. They settled down, to some degree. I think they came to realize that God was with Moses and us. When the plagues began we weren't effected by them?"

"I didn't know that."

"That's one of the many miracles. You would think we would have suffered just like everyone else. But when God took us to Egypt He arranged for Pharaoh to have us set apart in our own portion of the land, the portion called Goshen. It was because we were shepherds and that was odious to the Egyptians so he sent us off, out of their sight and mind. That's where we lived the rest of the time. We would go into Egypt or wherever we were sent after the edict was issued that we become slaves, but we always went back to Goshen at night, at least most of us did. Our families and our lives were there.

"At first, I don't think the Egyptians noticed that we weren't being afflicted. We were only afflicted if we were working in their part of the country but in Goshen, nothing bad was coming against us other than the Egyptians. At night, when we returned to our homes, the insects or whatever the current plague was seemed to fall off of us as we entered into our territory. It was miraculous. I know I keep saying that but it was all miraculous. Even now, it's a miracle."

"But Softa, you are leaving. How is that miraculous? How are we to get along without you?"

"Don't worry. God always provides. He'll hold your hand and walk you through the darkness and you'll be fine." Miriam paused, reaching out to her beloved granddaughter and resting her hand on Sarah's shoulder. She smiled at her and pulled her closer to her, embraced her and held her there for a moment. She thought about when she was a little girl and how she'd sit on her own grandmother's lap and they'd talk. It seemed as though nothing had changed, but everything had changed.

"Now, let's continue. Where was I? Oh yes, the plagues. The plagues were really terrifying, even if we weren't subjected to them. We heard about them. We heard about them everywhere and our people would come back to our villages and tell us about them. We were worried. We were worried that if the Egyptians found out that we weren't being affected by the plagues they would take revenge so it was decided that we wouldn't talk about it outside of our villages, outside of Goshen. We were told by the Council of Elders to keep quiet. They said if the Egyptians brought it up we were to sympathize with them and listen but not ever tell that we weren't experiencing them."

"Why do you think that was? That you weren't experiencing them?"

Miriam smiled and nodded her head. "At first, we didn't understand it. Then Moses and Aaron pointed out to us that each plague was a direct affront to a specific Egyptian god. Since these weren't our gods and since our God is the one true God and much more powerful than theirs, it was appropriate that we weren't affected. It was a war of the gods and ours was and is stronger.

"Eventually the Egyptians caught on. That was hard. They were even angrier than they had been before. They threatened us with all kinds of retaliation but nothing like that ever happened.

Some of the taskmasters became more difficult to work with, beating our people for no reason and killing some of them. It was sad. But it was also a witness to us that our God had everything under control and that, in spite of what we might think, He was taking care of us. At times that was pretty hard to believe."

"Were you scared?"

"Sometimes. But you have to remember that I had the gift of prophecy and I could see us – literally see us – leaving. I didn't know when. But I knew we would leave and that we would all go out together. Still, I didn't know how much longer our people would be willing to put up with the increased work load or if they would even be able to continue physically. That was frightening for them as well as for me. Yet, somehow I knew just to trust. Trust Him. Trust God. Trust Moses.

"It took a couple of months for the plagues to get severe enough for Pharaoh to even begin to consider letting us go. It didn't happen quickly. Each time, Pharaoh would command his magicians to stop the specific plague and make it go away. After several days, when they couldn't stop it, he would call Moses in and demand he stop the plague.

"Each time, Moses said, 'Let my people go!' Pharaoh would agree to it on the condition that Moses would pray to his God and lift the plague. Moses would pray and the plague would lift then Pharaoh would change his mind and say we couldn't go. Then there was the standoff as well. Moses wanted all of us to go. Men, women, children, animals, possessions – everything. Pharaoh was only willing to let a few of the men go. Each time he would relent a little more but generally he wouldn't agree to everything Moses was asking and that was the reason for the increase in plagues. Each time the plague became more severe, more pointed. It was like God was going up the chain against the Egyptian gods and Pharaoh would rebel and say no."

"What do you think was going on with him at the time? Why was he so stubborn?"

"I don't know. No one really knew. We all thought it was his advisors. You know, the people you surround yourself with have a great deal of influence on you and I think that's what it was with Pharaoh. Since it was a battle of the gods and so many of his advisors worshipped these gods, they couldn't accept the idea that their god would have to bow down and submit to ours. I'm not sure that's what it was but it was as good of an understanding as any. God never told me exactly what the reason was nor did I come to an understanding in a night vision so I just accepted it. Everyone did."

"What was it like that last day?"

"It was sad. Really sad. For a lot of reasons. I knew in the spirit that we were going. We knew what to expect, as much as we could. Moses and Aaron had done a good job of instructing us. From the very beginning, Moses had told us that our deliverance from bondage would be at the cost of the lives of Egypt's firstborn. That week, Moses called us, the family and the Tribal leaders all together and told us what to do. He had heard from God and He said it was time. We knew what we should expect and be prepared for.

"We were each - that is each family - to choose a lamb out of our flocks. It had to be perfect in every way. No blemishes. We were to choose it on the 10th day of Nissan and keep it near us until the 14th day of the month. That was to give us time to make sure no blemish or anything unclean would come against the animal and make it unworthy of being the ultimate sacrifice. But it also meant that we were going to become personally attached to the lamb as well. You see, a sacrifice that costs you nothing means nothing. We finally came to understand that as one of the reasons for having the lamb with us for that short time.

"The lamb had to be the right size for our family to consume as nothing could be left over. If it was too big for our family then we were to share it with another family. If anything was left over then it had to be destroyed in the fire."

"Why was that?"

"It was a covenant meal and only we Hebrews were to participate in it. Adonai was very specific about it. I understood from the very beginning. I got it. He was not only specific about how it was to be cooked – roasted actually; but, He was also specific about the way we were to eat it. We were to be ready to go at a moment's notice. We were to have our walking shoes on, fully clothed with cloaks and staffs and everything. Bags packed and wagons loaded. There would be no delay. When that trump was blown we were to set out immediately.

"And, as if that wasn't enough we were to take blood from the sacrificed lamb, dip hyssop in it and paint it on our doorposts so the death angel would know not to stop there. We were to paint the *Tav*, the symbol for truth, on the doorposts."

"But you were all set apart, in the land of Goshen. Wouldn't that have been enough?"

"You would think so but once it was discovered that we were immune to the plagues other people, Egyptians, started moving into Goshen. I don't know if they thought it was the location that made us immune or what, but sure enough, they started moving to Goshen. By then, we had a number of Egyptian families living around us. Sometimes if felt like they were a plague and, believe me, they weren't immune to the plagues just because they had changed location. Our neighbors would be suffering from flies, frogs, boils and what have you while we were walking free. It made them very angry at us."

"What did they do?"

"They didn't actually do anything to us. They complained. They made bad gestures and called us names but they didn't do anything to us. They couldn't really. I think they were afraid that the taskmasters would make them take our places if they did anything to us physically so they just put up with it. But they were not kind about it.

"Actually, I hadn't thought of it before, but I wonder if that was what made them give up their silver and gold and clothes that night when we asked for them to do so. I thought there would be more resistance but maybe they caught on to the fact that something was up and that we would be leaving? I don't know. They didn't argue with us, they just handed over the things we asked for. I guess you could say that was another miracle. By then they were eager to get rid of us and our God." Miriam couldn't contain a chuckle.

Sarah laughed with her grandmother, imagining the haste with which the Egyptians surrendered what was asked of them. It was so odd that they would do that.

"So what happened that night? Were you scared?"

"No. I wasn't scared. Your *Saba* Caleb had made sure our children were with us so we knew they were safe. We talked to them and told them what was happening and not to be frightened if they heard strange noises outside. We explained it to them the best we could but they were still pretty young. They seemed to understand. Even so, when the death angel came through and we began hearing the screams of the Egyptians when they saw their oldest child die, it was hard. Sometimes it wasn't just the child. If one of the parents was a firstborn, or in some cases both of them, then that parent, or parents, died as well. You couldn't help but weep for them. It could have been different but their leaders wouldn't relent. It wasn't the people's fault but we always pay for the decisions of our leaders."

"How did Moses know to go to Pharaoh?"

"Actually he didn't go. He and Pharaoh had had an argument, another one of their many arguments. This one was particularly vile. Moses tried to tell him what would happen but Pharaoh hardened his heart and wouldn't hear of it. He told Moses to get out and that he didn't ever want to see him again. And he didn't. That night the shofar blew and we started moving out, just as instructed. We had been on our journey for a while, a few hours I think, when word reached us that Pharaoh's oldest child, the crown prince, had also died. That was why he and his army weren't chasing us. They were all in their homes dealing with their own grief. We just kept marching. We were happy to be going but sad for the Egyptians."

"I've forgotten, how long did it take you to get to the Yom Suph?"

"It took several days for us to get to the sea. We were pretty well organized. We had a make-shift army, be that as it was. But it was God that led us through the wilderness to the sea. We marched between the mountains, in the *wadis* because they were dry and not such rugged terrain for the older ones, and the little ones too. We marched for several days following the cloud and the pillar of fire. The miraculous thing was that we didn't get tired, we just kept moving. We always had watchmen that trailed behind to make sure we weren't being followed and Moses sent men on ahead as well. We were happy and somewhat light hearted even though the going was rough.

"Several times we went back over the trail we had already covered. I'm sure if we were being watched they probably thought we were lost but we weren't." Miriam's eyes gave off a mysterious twinkle, making her look mischievous. "I think Adonai wanted it to look that way, to confuse Pharaoh because He knew Pharaoh would try, one more time, to destroy us. The truth is, there was one more Egyptian god that hadn't been dealt with, the one at Pithom, one of the cities that our people had been forced to build. Every time we built a new city the Egyptians would dedicate it to one of their gods and declare that deity as the god of that city. This god was Baal-Zephon. It had to be dealt with so the Egyptians couldn't say that he led the nations astray and he destroyed us.

"We knew the way to that city very well. Our people had gone there time and time again during its construction. We definitely were not lost. We were in a holding pattern that made it look like we were confused and wandering aimlessly, but we weren't. When we arrived there we did so by going between two large, upright rocks that looked somewhat like lips. It was as though we going through an open mouth to get to that location. Perhaps we were. Perhaps it was the mouth of God as He was the one that was fighting Pharaoh. Anyway, it was there that the showdown would happen. At Pithom, right in front of the Yom Suph.

"As to the Egyptian god, Baal–Zephon, that had yet to be dealt with, there could have been no better place. Baal-Zephon was their god of weather, or so they thought. I'm sure when they saw the cloud leading us and the pillar of fire following us that they must have thought their god was going to destroy us. But they didn't understand. It wasn't their god leading us, it was ours! When the showdown came it was our God and His cloud that held them back and kept them away from us.

"Once we got to the sea we were trying to figure out what to do. We thought we would have to build boats to get across and the men were trying to figure that one out when there was a shout from the watchmen. At first they thought it was a storm coming after us because of the roar and the dust cloud. Then they realized it wasn't a storm, at least not a weather storm. It was Pharaoh and his army, all six hundred chariots and horsemen. We were terrified. Our backs were to the sea. The mountains that we had just come through were in front of us. We were trapped. There was nowhere to go."

"What happened? I know what happened, but what happened. This is such a great story and I love hearing it."

"God happened! Everyone was terrified. They were screaming at Moses telling him to do something, questioning if he had brought us out of Egypt to let us die here. They even asked if there weren't enough graves in Egypt that we would have to die in this place. It was unsettling.

"But Moses wasn't afraid. He knew what to do. He said to the people, 'Have no fear! Stand by and witness the deliverance which the Lord will work for you today. The Egyptians who you see rushing towards you today, you'll never see again. The Lord will battle for you. Hold your peace!'

"They didn't understand that God would be vindicated that day. It was Pharaoh that had sentenced us into slavery for his glory. He never took into consideration that we were the people of God, chosen by Him for His service, not Pharaoh's. When Pharaoh forced us to do his bidding, God determined He would not only set us free but He would be glorified and vindicated in doing so. The battle was God's, from the very beginning.

"All of it was a part of God's plan, just as it was when our ancestors sold Joseph into slavery. It was he who had made a provision for us without his knowing, yet when our forefathers arrived in Egypt he knew the prophecy he had been given as a youth was being walked out. Even so, when our forefathers went down to Egypt to escape the famine, we were only seventy people strong. Now, two hundred and thirty years later, we had grown into a huge nation, well over a million strong if you include those under the age of twenty in the count. Just getting us organized and out of Goshen had been a huge task, then keeping us marching had been a challenge. I don't know if it would have happened if it hadn't been for the angel that helped lead us and the cloud and pillar of fire that we could see, day and night.

"The cloud that had been traveling with us by day suddenly became a dark, forbidding pillar of God's fury. The angel of God, Metatron, that had been traveling with us grabbed the pillar of cloud and moved around behind us standing in the way of Pharaoh and his chariots like a giant wall. They couldn't get past it because it was roaring and twirling and destroying anything that came near it. We were mesmerized just watching it. There was a lot of noise coming from the cloud and the screams of the people.

"I'm not sure how he could hear, but Moses did hear the voice of God and he lifted his staff motioning for the people to be quiet. Then he turned and pointed his staff toward the Yom Suph and the waters started moving backwards. It was amazing. They moved backwards in giant rocking waves, then they parted completely making a channel for us to go through. At first, I didn't know if we could do it because it was so muddy but the moment the first foot lifted, that of Nachshon, the prince of the Tribe of Judah, and started to step on the mud it dried out and we went across on dry land! Miraculous."

Miriam paused, remembering the moment of their deliverance from Pharaoh and from Egypt. Her thoughts seemed to be far away as though she were there that very moment. The vision of that day rolled through her memory. She shivered.

"The power of the cloud and its fury was not the only miracle that was happening. At the same time, the pillar of fire was leading the way for us. It went before us providing both light and direction. There would be no confusion on which way to go. We followed the light of the fire and we moved forward.

"It was wonderful! They started across carrying the bones of Joseph and a calm settled over the people. Moses reminded them to hurry, not to dawdle as they crossed as it was a long walk. It was a very long walk and we needed to go as quickly as possible. Some of the guys carried children on their backs as well as packs. They led animals across that were hitched to buggies carrying the elderly and overloaded with belongings. It was a huge undertaking.

"It took hours for our people to get across the dry bed of the Yom Suph but they made it. No one fell. No one ran out of energy. Just as God had sustained our energy during the preceding days, he sustained it now. We moved forward as though it were easy but there was no way it should have been easy. It was as though He carried us on His wings.

"All the time, we were aware that Pharaoh and his army were on the other side of that wall of cloud. We were afraid that they might break through at any moment. The trumpeters kept sounding the horns, moving the people forward as quickly as possible. A couple of the men picked up tubs, stretched fabric across them like a drum and started beating out a cadence trying to make it easier for the people to keep up the pace. The ground was dry but it was rough and there was debris there from the sea, sea weed and stuff that could cause people to stumble. But we kept going and going and going. Finally, they made it across with the bones of Joseph and then they came back to help others across.

"Moses was everywhere. I don't know how that happened. He was on the bank of the sea. He was on a high rock in the middle of the sea. His staff was in the air and his hands were outstretched. He was magnificent. He hurried the people on. He called them by their names, encouraging them and telling them they could do it, they were almost there. It was amazing!"

Miriam's voice thundered with excitement at the remembrance of the journey across the dry sea bed. Her eyes sparkled as though streaks of lightening were being reflected in them. The very memory of the event sparked new excitement, life and an obvious joy in her.

"And the cloud held. It stood in that same spot, trapping Pharaoh and his army. It was almost like the cloud was laughing at the Egyptians. Then, as the last family made it across, the cloud began to slowly lift into the sky, like a giant gate being raised, to let Pharaoh through. As always, Pharaoh was in the lead with his soldiers following closely behind. They came in a rush, riding as fast as they could bringing death and destruction with them. As soon as the last chariot was on the dry sea bed, the floor became very wet and mud-like, bogging down the chariots and causing the wheels to come loose and fall off.

"Then God told Moses to stretch out his staff toward the Egyptians. He did. There was a mighty roar and the sea closed! It just closed like the unrolling of a scroll. We saw chariots tipping and sinking and bodies flaying in the waves then silently floating. Horses struggled to swim but drowned in the rush of the water, held down by the very chariots they were harnessed to. It was exciting. It was frightening.

"We understood Pharaoh was the one who initiated the sin against God by all he had done to us and he was the first to be caught up in the rushing, roaring waves. He was swept away by the tidal waves, drowned. He was gone. We were alive.

"The last we saw of them was a few stragglers that had managed to pull themselves from the water onto the bank on the far side of the sea, the Egyptian side. They stared at the sea like it was alive, and it was. It had just eaten up Pharaoh and his army, yet we were free."

"What did you do? How did that feel?"

"It was wonderful. It was sad to see so many people die but they could have lived had they chosen a different path. Instead they rode with a furious hate in their hearts, determined to kill and capture us and return us to slavery. Now they were gone. Almost all of them. They wouldn't be bothering us again and that was a great thing to understand.

"Moses broke into song. I don't think any of us had realized how much pressure he had been under these months. You know, it takes a lot of courage to stand before Pharaoh and make the declarations that he had made and then to have to deal with us. It was a huge task but he rose to it."

"You said he sang. What was the song that he sung?"

"You know it. We sing it a lot."

"Oh yes, this one,
'I will sing to the LORD, for He is highly exalted;
The horse and its rider he has hurled into the sea.
The LORD is my strength and song,
And He has become my salvation;
This is my God, and I will praise Him;
My father's God, and I will extol Him.'"

"Yes, that one. I love it." The two of them started humming the song together then they stopped, looked at each other and laughed.

"I couldn't help myself. If my brother was going to show off his musical abilities I would as well. I grabbed a tambourine from a friend standing next to me and I started dancing. It was like joy had come all over me, washing me in a light heartedness that I had never experienced before. We had been through so much and now we saw all of the anguish we had suffered, washed into the sea. It was amazing. We had been redeemed."

"When you started dancing, was Moses still singing?"

"Yes, he was. He looked at me and smiled then he broke into laughter. It was the first time I had seen him laugh since he was a little boy. Now he laughed. I cried and laughed and danced and sang. It was wonderful."

"What were you singing?"

"It was the chorus to what Moses was singing,

"'Sing to the LORD, for He is highly exalted.
The horse and his rider He has hurled into the sea."

"It caught on like a wildfire. The other women grabbed their tambourines and we were all singing and dancing and rejoicing in the Lord. We had just come through a nightmare and we were free. We didn't know what lay ahead but we were free and we wanted to celebrate our freedom. We had a party right there on the banks of the sea. People dropped the burdens they had carried across that span of dry sea bed and lifted their hands and hearts to rejoice.

"We stayed there for several days. The fear was gone. Gone with the drowning of Pharaoh and his army. Moses had to get us organized and that took a while. But, at that point we could afford the luxury of time. No one was chasing us. No one was forcing us to work for them. We were truly free. For some of us, that was almost too much.

"Almost immediately, the people began to complain. Mostly about silly things that didn't matter. Where were they going to sleep? What were they going to eat? We had plenty of stuff with us to keep us for a while, in fact the food we brought out of Egypt lasted us nearly six weeks. I think they were just unnerved because they were free and they didn't know how to act as free people. They needed to have someone tell them what to do. That was all they had known for several generations. Moses got us organized into our tribes, reestablishing the original Twelve Tribes. Then called a meeting with the tribal leaders, the Council. It was the beginning of the moving on.

"While we had a new found sense of freedom, I don't think we understood then that we weren't really free. We still are not free, not even now. You see, we, as a people, won't be really free until we cross over into the Promised Land and take it as ours, just as God has instructed us to do. Then, when we've taken the land and cleared it of the enemy, then we'll be free. We are on our way now, closer than we've been in thirty-nine years, but we aren't there yet."

Six—The Rock

They took another break to give themselves time to adjust to the emotion of the story. It was intense, but it was delightfully fulfilling remembering all that God had brought them through. Even though the soon departure of Miriam loomed over them they found great joy in the telling of the story. When they came back together they were both refreshed and even eager to get on with the telling.

Once again, Miriam stoked the fire. She wasn't cold from the external temperature, in fact the desert was comfortably warm but not overly hot at this time of year. She just enjoyed the fire, the glow and the smell of the burning coals were comforting. It reminded her of so much and made it easier to carry on with the memories which were as tentative as the wood that was being consumed by the fire. She knew she had to finish the telling. She wanted to finish.

They settled down together, leaning back on the couch-bed and looking into the depth of the fire. Miriam began again, "That was when I first noticed the rock. We had crossed the Yom Suph the day before and celebrated most of the night. As the morning sun was rising I was wandering around taking in the freedom of being on this side of the sea. I was walking along the shoreline, wondering at the awe of everything that had happened."

"The rock? Is that where you got it? How did you know it would be the source of water?"

"I didn't know. While we were there on this side of the Yom Suph, the free side, I started paying attention to the things that had washed up from the sea. Like everyone else I picked up a few elements from Pharaohs army, now drowned. I picked up a couple of leather shields that had somehow floated to the surface and I even found a spear. I noticed an odd rock, so odd in fact that I picked it up and brought it back to our tent with me.

"When your *Saba* Caleb came in later that morning, I was showing him all of my finds, including the rock. He, too, thought it was odd. It looked almost like a large sea sponge. It was nearly that same camel color. It had holes in it yet it was very heavy. We couldn't figure it out but I was attracted to it and wanted to keep it. We talked about it and he thought it was alright to keep it until we started marching again then I would probably have to leave it behind because it was so heavy even though it wasn't that large. I understood his thoughts and agreed with him.

"Over the next couple of days, while we were still there on the shore, I noticed that the rock was always wet. I thought that was odd. I would move it out to the sun and let it dry out but when I moved it back into the tent it was wet again. That was so abnormal. I sat the rock in a bowl, just to keep it from creating a muddy mess on the dirt floor and the next thing I knew the bowl was full of fresh, clean water. That was strange. So strange, in fact, that it kind of bothered me.

"We carefully sampled the water, expecting it to be salty since the rock appeared to have come from the Yom Suph, but the water was fresh and very drinkable. It tasted good, refreshing and very satisfying. We were faced with the dilemma of trying to figure this all out, but really we had no answers.

"I began playing a game with the rock. I would move it from spot to spot. I would put it in various bowls or buckets. The same thing happened again and again. The rock was making water. I didn't understand it. I played with it. Moved it and repeated it. Always there was the rock and there was water. We figured out that if I was near the rock, it would give off more water. If I left and was in another part of the camp, then the rock would barely seep water. When I came back, it would quickly fill the bowl or pitcher or whatever it was in. It was almost like it was happy to see me which we both thought was very strange. A rock doesn't have feelings so how could it be happy or sad depending on my coming and going?

"*Saba* Caleb and I talked about it. We tested it. We watched it. We tried to figure it out. Was it a fluke or was this something significant that we needed to pay attention to. Finally, he said he needed to tell Moses about it. While he was gone to talk to Moses I asked God to see if I could get an answer. I didn't hear anything specific but in my spirit I knew this was no ordinary rock and for whatever reason I needed to keep it close to me. We didn't yet understand the full significance of the rock but I knew it was connected to me and would be remaining at my side, at least for now.

"When *Saba* Caleb came back from his talk with Moses, he told me how he had explained it all to my brothers and their reactions. He said both Moses and Aaron were very interested in the rock and its output and that they would come by later to check it out. They asked a lot of questions about the rock and wondered how we would manage to take it with us since it was so heavy, yet the water content was extremely important, especially considering the fact that we were headed into the Negev. He said they went over all kinds of ideas and asked him to look into it and to come back to them with some ideas on moving it. They would come by to see it before we set out on our journey.

"The funny thing is, they didn't ask me. I was beginning to get answers from God, slowly at first but over the next couple of days I received the understanding. You know how it works. You've watched it so many times and you've seen me position the rock so it will provide water for everyone."

"Yes, I have watched you and several times I've even helped you. I still don't understand it though. How does it happen? What makes it work?"

"I don't know. I can only say 'God!' I do know that when I've been singing and dancing before the Lord, the water is more abundant, almost like a rushing spring. At first that presented problems because it would overflow and flood everything in our tent, causing a huge mess. Then we began to understand it better and to know how to handle it."

"But when you raise it high on a pedestal it makes more water. How did you know to do that?"

"Like I know how to do anything. We continued experimenting with the rock. As long as we were at Yom Suph it wasn't any big deal. It was just a wet rock, but when we started the journey going deep into the wilderness where there isn't much water, the rock became more significant. When we would stop at places where there was no water, I would feel led of the Lord to take the rock near the center of the encampment and place it on a pillar. Then I would take a heavy stick and drag channels, not deep ones, but channels towards the tribes. I would drag twelve channels out away from the rock, like wheel spokes, and water would start to flow. It would run along the desert floor and when it got to the various tribes it would be wet, but dirty.

"The people weren't happy with this. They wanted fresh water and they were upset that Moses wasn't supplying it for them. We had been traveling three days from the Yom Suph when we camped at Marah. There was water there but it was bitter, nasty tasting and some of the people said it gave them a stomach ache. This made the people mad. They didn't want to drink the bitter water because it would make them sick but they didn't drink from the water of the rock either as they didn't want dirty water."

"What happened?"

"God told Moses to throw a tree into the bitter waters of Marah. He did. The water became fresh and clean and the people drank it. They didn't trust my rock and they didn't think it could provide enough water for everyone so when the waters of Marah became fresh, they were happy. At least for the moment.

"We moved on from there to Elim. We saw the oasis from a distance and were excited to hear when our forerunners came back with the report that there were twelve springs of what we thought would be beautifully fresh water as indicated by the seventy date palm trees. When we first saw the trees and the water, we thought we had arrived in the Promised Land and I wondered why I had this rock. We were all so happy and we looked forward to camping and resting there for a few days. But the water wasn't as abundant as we thought it would be and the trees were scraggly and sickish.

"Even so, when Moses told us to move on there was a protest but it didn't do any good. The people were willing to settle there because they thought the water would sustain them. But it wasn't enough to do that for very long. The cloud stood ready to move and we had to follow. It was obvious that we were going deeper into the desert and everyone was troubled by that. Water would be an issue and we all knew it. I was beginning to understand why I had the rock although I did not understand why I was the one chosen to be attached to it.

"No one wanted dirty water and I couldn't blame them. We had to figure out another solution. I came up with the idea that I would raise the rock on a pillar and women from the tribes would come with their jugs and draw water from the rock. That worked. Everyone seemed to be happy about that and I was delighted to have been chosen keeper of the rock, if you will. Soon people began referring to the rock as living water. It did bring life, there is no doubt about that."

They both laughed. "Maybe I should make you an apron that says 'rock keeper'" Sarah said. Then she suddenly got quiet. "I guess that won't be much good as you would probably be gone before I got the apron made."

"Well, I'll be gone before I get this story finished if I don't get on with it. Let's continue. The odd thing about the rock is that it only seems to work with me. I've never really understood that. When your *Saba* Caleb put the rock on the pillar, nothing would happen. It just dripped a little but that was all. For whatever reason, I had to be the one to care for the rock, to allow it to move along with me and to place it on the pillar in order for it to provide adequate refreshment for the tribes. I guess you could say it became my responsibility at a time when we were all looking for understanding of who we were and what it was that God wanted with us."

"About that, Softa. What happens to the rock when you leave? We haven't reached the Promised Land yet and we are all dependent on that rock. Will it go with you? Do you know?"

"I have no idea. I've wondered about that myself. You know we can't take anything with us when we go into The Light so I don't imagine it will go. But I don't know what will happen here. Maybe Adonai will anoint you as the keeper of the rock."

"I think I would be honored to do that but with my tent so full of little ones, I don't know where I'd put it. And, knowing them, they'd think it was their own toy and it could create problems."

"I don't know what is going to happen to the rock. I assume it will continue providing for everyone just as it has these almost forty years. It hasn't failed us yet. God hasn't failed us although we've failed Him so many times."

"Have you ever wondered if the rock is a symbol of something bigger than you or me or any of us? Is there more to it than that?"

"I've wondered a lot of things about it. I don't have the answers. I know the rock provides. I have had the sense that when we sing songs unto Adonai and worship Him, the rock is renewed. But I don't know that. I just sense that. Sometimes when I wash my hair in its water or wash my body, I have the sense that it is something very special – almost holy. I don't know but I can say I'm thankful for the rock and its provision."

"I've seen you with the rock so many times that I've taken it for granted. I've never really understood how it moved from one place to another though."

"I've never really understood it either. At first, we tried to carry the rock but it would get so heavy that it was requiring several men to take turns carrying it and they would get soaked. That was alright on hot days but they didn't like being wet in the cold desert nights. Next they tried to figure out how to carry it in a sling on a pole suspended between two men but the rock apparently didn't like that. It wouldn't give us any water on those days. I don't know if it was because I wasn't near it or what. *Saba* Caleb tried building a wagon of sorts for the rock but that wasn't successful. Again, the rock didn't seem to like the wagon and the wagon quickly disintegrated leaving the rock on its own.

"I was praying and asking the Lord what we should do. How were we supposed to get the rock from one location to another? There didn't seem to be a clear way to do it without causing all kinds of issues yet we couldn't leave the rock where it was. We needed it, desperately."

"So what happened? I don't remember ever seeing you carry the rock or anything yet it is always with you, or at least it is near."

Miriam smiled and thought about Sarah's question. 'What did happen?' she wondered? She couldn't remember when she actually knew that the rock would move on its own, but she had come to that understanding early on. From there, things had gotten much easier, at least as far as the rock was concerned.

"What happened? God happened. Somehow I knew that the rock was not a problem that it would come with me and be with me – us - wherever I went. I had to put my trust in that and be willing to move on without worrying about how the rock would get there and just relax. It never failed to show up wherever I was. Strange? Yes, very strange. Miraculous? Most definitely."

"How did people react to your traveling rock?" Sarah asked, her eyes twinkling with mirth. "Were they laughing?"

"Sure they laughed, at first. But you know, when we would get to one of our locations and there wasn't any visible source of water, the laughter stopped. Once we figured out to put the rock on the pedestal and it flowed out abundantly, they would come with their jugs and get water. In the end, it worked out very well for everyone. We were all mesmerized by it but we came to accept it as a miraculous gift from God."

Seven—Manna

"I was thinking this morning, before you came, that this entire journey has been one miracle after another. But, it has also been a journey of learning and judgment. Many times we made huge mistakes. If they were just that, mistakes, God used them as an opportunity to teach us through Moses. If they were incidents of sin or rebellion, then judgment rained down on us from the heavens with fire and brimstone and the full fury of God.

"It wasn't long after we came out of Egypt, about six weeks I think, that the people began complaining because we were running out of food. It was reasonable, in my opinion, that they became frightened even though we had learned by then that God was taking us through impossible situations by His miracles. Each time He met our needs.

"Had we been thinking correctly, we would have known He would meet this need as well. But when you see the food dwindling and you have children to feed, parental instincts kick in. You know that as a parent.

"We had gone through the experience of the bad water at Marah and how God sweetened it with the tree. We had gone through the experience of the Oasis at Elim, where we thought there would be water in abundance just from the existence of the seventy palm trees but we didn't realize until we got up close to them that the water supply was not adequate even for them. The palm trees were weak, spindly, and not producing, all from a lack of sufficient water. Suddenly well over a million people show up, with their animals, and we expect to have enough water. It wasn't going to work and the people grumbled once again.

"They complained to Moses, saying, 'If only we had died by the hand of the Lord in Egypt, when we had pots of meat and ate bread to our fill. But no, you have brought us out into this desert to starve us to death, all of us with no food and no water!' They never seemed to quit with that ridiculous assertion.

"It was hard on Moses. He had given up so much for all of us and there didn't seem to be any gratitude from anyone. I know he felt as though he were alone in this responsibility but he did have the assurance that God had told him to lead us. Once again, he went before God with the people's complaints and, once again, God answered in a magnificent way. He said, 'Listen. I am going to rain bread down for you from heaven and the people shall go out and gather what is needed each day. It is my test of them to see if they are willing to follow my teaching. Each day, there will be enough bread for that day except for the sixth day when I will rain down twice as much. They are to collect one *omer* for each member of their family, no more. On the sixth day, they are to collect twice that amount for they are not allowed to work on the seventh day. I will see if they trust me.'"

"Do you think the people didn't trust God? Is that what this was all about?"

"Trust is a difficult thing. Sometimes it comes slowly. We have to learn that we can trust. As for you and your generation, you've always known God's provision. You've lived your entire life on this desert, marching along with us. You didn't know the food and the comfort of Egypt like my generation did. And, you didn't know the discomfort and the terror of slavery either. For you, trust is easy. For us, we had to learn it. This was one of God's ways of teaching us to trust Him, through His daily provision.

"But the people continued to grumble. God heard them and He told Moses to tell the people 'I have heard the complaints of the children of Israel. Tell them in the afternoon you shall eat meat and in the morning you shall be satisfied with bread and you shall know that I am God.'"

"But how could they not know? Everything that has happened up to this point, He has directed, guided, answered and provided. How could they keep doubting?"

"You have to remember, we had just come out of Egypt. When we were there, even though we were slaves, everything was provided for us. The food. Our clothes. The houses we lived in. Everything. We didn't have to pay for anything. It was all furnished. In turn, we owed Egypt everything, including our lives and our obedience. It sounds good, but it wasn't. Sometimes, it is easy to forget the bad and remember the good parts, especially if you don't know what to expect from the future. None of us knew what to expect. We had Moses and we had God through Moses and Aaron and that was all. Trust? That had to be learned.

"Sure enough, that night we had quail. Everyone was so excited. They didn't care where it came from. It was meat. Delicious, delicate meat. The quail were flying by, low to the ground, as was their custom at this time of year. We didn't realize any of this. We saw them land in droves to rest and we pounced on them, captured them, killed them and ate. It was wonderful and everyone was so happy. I think they, the people, were actually encouraged by it all.

"The next morning, just as Moses had promised, we had bread. You've seen how it happens. The dew comes down and replenishes the plants and what vegetation there is. When the dew lifts there is all of the white stuff that looks like coriander seed, the same seed we often used in cooking in Egypt. We didn't know what to make of it or what to call it. We asked, 'what is this' so many times that it became its name, manna, which means 'what is this?'

"At first, we gathered more than an *omer* a piece as we didn't know what to expect. There was enough for us to gather all we wanted and believe me, we did. What we didn't know was that the next morning it would be disgusting. Overnight, what hadn't been eaten, turned to maggots and worms and smelled like rotten eggs. It was horrible. Repulsive. We had to throw it out. Cleaning the pots was a messy thing, but we had to do it and with a limited supply of water. We learned. That was the point. We were supposed to learn to trust God for our daily provision.

"We also learned how to cook manna. I know, you love it. So do I. But we didn't love it at first. Once we got past the 'what is this stuff' stage, we set about learning about it. Actually, it was almost magical in the sense it became almost anything you wanted it to be. If your taste buds were hungry for fish, then it would taste like fish. If for something else, say cheese, then it would taste like cheese. And the women became very good at discovering ways of fixing it and making it into superb dishes, like those you and I have experienced today. It truly was and is a blessing.

"That lasted for a while, quite a while actually. But there is always someone that has to find fault and complain and that was what happened. We had been on the journey for two years by then, you were just a little thing so I don't know if you remember any of this or not. Some of the Egyptians that had been traveling with us began complaining. I don't know if they were bored or what. But, they started hollering and complaining about Moses and his leadership, about the way things were being done and so on.

"We had just settled down and set up camp after a three day march when their complaining started again. God heard it and He answered, immediately, with fire which ravaged the outskirts of the camp! The people panicked, cried out to Moses and he interceded with God and stopped the fire. It seemed they would never learn and they didn't learn then.

"They complained again, the riff raff that had come with us from Egypt. This time they were tired of manna. They wanted meat. Real meat. Not imaginary meat. They were crying out for and demanding the cucumbers, leeks and garlic of Egypt. And, oh yes, the melons too. They hated the manna. They lined up in front of the Tent of Meeting and complained, non-stop. Moses was frustrated. He went to God and said he'd had enough of these people; that they weren't what he signed up for.

"That was when God told Moses to gather seventy elders from the tribes and to bring them to the Tent of Meeting, on the outskirts of the encampment. From now on, they were to assist Moses in dealing with people like this and their endless complaints. God put some of the same spirit that was on Moses on these seventy men so they could help with the people. Then He told Moses to tell the people to purify themselves because the next day they would have meat.

"He reiterated to them their complaining and then promised them that they wouldn't have meat for just one day but for thirty days! He said they would eat meat until it came out of their nostrils!"

"Ugh! What a grotesque thought!"

"Yes, it is. But what happened next wasn't any better. He promised them that they would have so much meat that they would get sick of it. Well, they got it! This time God caused a huge wind to blow in from the sea. At first, it felt good even though it stirred up a lot of dirt. With the wind came quail from the sea. There were so many quail that they were two cubits deep in the camp and a day's journey on either side of it. There were thousands of quail, all dropping right here in our laps.

"They gathered quail all that day, all that night and into the next day. Every one gathered the quail, except our family. By then, we had learned to love the manna but we were willing to eat the quail. Still, we had a funny feeling about it and I was very hesitant to bring it into our tent. Something didn't feel right about it.

"As it turned out, my intuition was right. Before the people even had their first full meal of quail, God's anger was unleashed on us. People were still chewing the meat when suddenly a plague hit and they started dying, without warning. The plague was severe and a lot of people died that day, so many that Moses named the place Kibroth-Hattaavah, meaning 'the graves of craving'. It was frightening. It taught us that we needed to be careful about what we ask for as sometimes we get it! That was hard."

Eight—Stones

"Softa, what about the stones. The second set, the ones with the Ten Sayings that survived all of the things that happened? Tell me about that."

"Ah yes, I can't leave those out. That entire story is so intriguing. Our people had already established a legitimate relationship with the One True God before we ever went into Egypt, you know, to escape the famine when Father Jacob took us down there. In fact, that was one of the main reasons he didn't want to go to Egypt because he knew they worshipped idols and Pharaoh as god and he didn't want our family subjected to idol worship of any kind.

"But, the famine got so bad that they had to go down for food and that was when it was discovered that Joseph was alive, living in Egypt and had, in fact, become second in command to Pharaoh. As a youth he had prophesied that his brothers and his parents would bow down to him someday. In fact that was one of the things that got him into so much trouble with his brothers and caused them to sell him to a caravan of Midianites who, in turn, sold him to the Egyptians. Without the brothers realizing it, they had put Joseph into position for the prophecies to be walked out. By stationing Joseph in Egypt, second to Pharaoh, it was obvious that God had made provision for our family long before the famine set in. No one had any idea what would happen when they went down there. It was supposed to be for a short time, a temporary reprieve.

"However, with Joseph alive and in charge and the Egyptians being so kind to our family, it became too easy not to just settle in and live there. It was three generations before Pharaoh's edict came forth to kill the boy babies and that started the entire exodus although no one knew it at the time.

"During those three generations, our people had begun to assimilate with the Egyptian culture although it was not generally accepted. Some of our people were inner-marrying which only created more confusion as to how the children would be raised; as Egyptians or as Hebrews. God did need to do something to get us out of that land and on our way home. However, no one ever thought He would allow something so tremendously terrible to happen as Pharaoh's edict.

"Like I told you before, once Moses was adopted by Princess *Bithiah* the edict just faded away. The main thing we had to contend with was the increase in slavery and the assimilation that was going on. It was time to go and go we did.

"Once we stepped into freedom our faith in the One True God had to be renewed and brought back to its righteousness. Every time Moses went up on the mountain to meet with God, it was to bring a message of righteousness back to our people. As you know, while he was in the presence of God our people were running amuck and acting like Egyptians on a religious holiday. It was pretty sad. Pathetic, really.

"The first time Moses came down from the mountain he had the two stones with him which held the Ten Sayings, hand carved and written by God, with His own finger, on them. What was intended as a wonderful encouragement, reminder and even a beautiful piece of artwork, if you will, was smashed to nothing by the anger of Moses when he saw what had happened with the Golden Calf.

"There are just not enough words to describe the despair that we felt. Oh not all of us, but some of us. We were devastated. Here Moses was after forty days of being on the mountain in the presence of God to come down to something like the debauchery that was going on. Worst of all was the fact that Aaron had allowed it to happen, that he somehow had failed to put a stop to it. Maybe it was because Joshua wasn't with us, but had gone part way up the mountain with Moses. I don't know why Aaron didn't stop it, but he didn't.

"So here is Moses with all of this awe and joy he had experienced in the presence of the Lord only to have it destroyed by what he witnessed down below. In his anger he raised the Two

Stones – the Ten Sayings – above his head and smashed them to the ground breaking them into hundreds of pieces.

"After he dealt with Aaron and the rebel rousers, he had to repent before God for the destruction of the Two Stones that he had smashed. But he also had to stop God from destroying all of us, which is what God really wanted to do. It was a huge struggle and a lot of pleading and interceding on Moses' part. Finally, he succeeded. Then he had to start over.

"I've already told you about the box Zipporah said he made. Well that box was for the broken pieces of the Two Stones. He went to the foothills of the mountain, fell on his knees and carefully picked up every cherished piece of those stones and put them in the box he had made. That box and those pieces of stone are still with us and they travel with us every time we break camp and start out. God has ordained that they stay with us as a reminder of what happened.

"After things settled down, Moses went back up on the mountain, but not before he had personally hand cut two more stones to carry up with him. It must have been hard climbing up there with the stones in his hands. I'm sure he was wondering what he would find this time when he came back down, but in his obedient nature he did as instructed and took the stones up with him. Once again, he was gone for forty days and nights.

"As before, we watched the mountain top and we saw the glow. We worried about his well-being but this time no one acted up. This time, it seemed everyone was walking around rather carefully, waiting to see what would happen when he came back down. And that was amazing.

"Not only did he have the Two Stones with him, completed as before, but his face actually glowed. We hadn't seen that before. It was stunning and shocking. It ended up with him having to put a veil over his face each time he came down from the mountain after that. He would remove it when he went up and then put it back on when he came down. This time though, he didn't smash the stones. He didn't have to. The people had managed to maintain a sense of dignity while he was gone and this time, Aaron kept them busy with various projects.

"They built the Ark of the Covenant according to God's instructions and placed the second set of stones in it. Now we had the Ten Sayings protected and in a place where they could be taken with us without worry as we moved from location to location.

"Essentially, the Ten Sayings are a shortened version of the 613 commandments that God has given us down through the ages. They are a quick reminder of our relationship with man and with Him. If we follow these Ten Sayings we will be able to live a life that is pleasing to Him, knowing they are the guide lines of deeper meaning and understanding. We should be grateful that we have them so close to us as reminders although we aren't allowed to see them or handle them. Still, we know they are there and that is good."

"I am thankful he kept the pieces as well. Anytime God writes something with His own finger it has to be holy. I hate to think of what might happen if another people came and picked up those pieces. Don't you think they would have some power to them – the pieces? They came directly from the finger of God. They have to be significant, don't they?" Sarah asked.

"I think so. I think anything that comes from God is significant if we will only stop and give it the proper place. I think every time we see a new baby born, a sunset, a sunrise, hear laughter, the list goes on and on, but it's all about God. We need to remember that and appreciate it for what it is instead of becoming so unaware of what is going on around us. I love the fact that God created a beautiful world for us, even this barren desert. I see beauty here, in the animals, in the flowers and the few trees. The mountains are exquisite and I never get tired of watching the shadows on the mountains change as the sun moves across the horizon. It's like a heavenly dance performed for those who will stop and watch. It's all from God and we should be grateful."

"I agree. I wish everyone would stop and look. We are all in such a hurry. Now that we are getting so close to the Promised Land everyone is excited about what is to be and not paying any attention to what is. That makes me sad. But, I understand."

"You are a sweet and tender spirit, my Sarah. You are a strong woman and you will lead your family though a great many wonderful events in the coming years. When you build your home in the Promised Land, your real home, keep this desert experience in your heart and mind. Sometimes the desert is harsh but it is here that we have become the People of God, the ones He chose us to be.

"Our people will face many challenges when they cross over into the land. Some will not be all that bad but others will be hard. If they will stay faithful to the One True God and listen, really listen, to what they are instructed to do by Him, they will be okay. Always make sure your family knows His word and follows it. You will be okay. I know that in my spirit."

Nine—Tzara'at

"I need to ask you something, Softa. Does *Saba* Caleb know you are leaving?"

"Yes, he does know. He was the first to know. I told him this morning, as soon as I knew."

"That must have been hard. What did he say?"

Miriam smiled, her eyes glistening. "I know you probably don't realize it, but *Saba* and I love each other very much. We've been through a great deal together. You ask what he did. He did the same thing you did. He cried. He hugged me. He said he didn't want me to go. But I think he's come to accept it now."

"Where is he? I thought he would be in here with you."

"No, he knew I wanted to talk to you. He went to talk to Moses and Aaron. They'll probably be here in a little while. I know they'll want to ask questions and to go over some things. You know, it's always been the three of us - Moses, Aaron and me - that God has used to work out His plan so we need to make sure we've accomplished what we were supposed to do. Or, I guess I should say that I've accomplished everything I was supposed to do since I'm the one that is leaving."

Sarah thought about that for a moment. "Do you want me to leave when they get here?"

"No, probably not. If they need you to leave I'll tell you. Until then, you can stay and that will be another thing for you to witness. But, we need to get on with the telling while we can. Once they get here I don't know how much time they'll take or how much time I'll have remaining to finish the story. Is there anything that you think you aren't clear on, that you need me to clarify for you?"

"I've never understood why you got into trouble with God. I've heard whispers about it but I don't know the story. Do you mind telling me that story?"

"It isn't something I like to talk about, I can tell you that. But it is something that needs to be told just so someone else doesn't do the same thing, make the same foolish mistake. I've never been so scared in my life, not before and not sense then and believe me, there were a lot of scary events in the last thirty-nine years, but that was the worst."

"What happened?"

"It was my fault. I should have handled things differently. The only reason I'm going to tell you about this now is so that you will teach it to your children and never make the same mistake. But, this is just between us now, okay? I'm still embarrassed and troubled by it. It was terrible."

"Softa, don't. If you don't want to tell me, that's okay."

"No. I need to tell you. You need to know and understand the truth of what really happened.

"It started with Zipporah, Moses wife. When he brought her back with him, from Midian, and the two little guys, Gershom and Eliezer, we were so excited. I immediately loved her. We just clicked. She was beautiful in every way. Not only was she physically beautiful, but she was beautiful on the inside as well. I thought she was very sophisticated, the daughter of a prince, and I loved her. We quickly became good friends and confidants.

"I knew she wasn't a Hebrew but I didn't care. So many things had happened to our people, from the time of the edict of Pharaoh to kill the babies and on, that I was willing to accept anyone that would accept us for whom we were and not try to kill us.

"From the very beginning, Zipporah seemed to be overwhelmed by it all. As I said, she came out of a good place of freedom and respect into the hideousness that had become Egypt and their treatment of us. As the wife of Moses, she was badly mistreated by the Egyptians. One time she was walking though the market trying to get food for her family when one of the merchants started calling her names and screaming at her. Soon there was a crowd of people surrounding her, pushing and

78

shoving. She was alone with the two boys and she was badly frightened.

"She ran back to our part of the community, crying and without food. Someone came and told me they saw her running and crying so I went in pursuit of her. I found her back in their house, sobbing so hard she could hardly tell me what had happened. We struggled in overcoming the language differences as it was and communication was hard, at best. Now that she was so upset we really struggled to get to the point of the matter.

"The boys were upset as well. I saw the empty food basket and began piecing things together. We communicated as well as we could and I figured out that the Egyptians were blaming her and her husband for the misery that had been brought down on them. It was very hard for her. Everything was new to her and then this happening, it was too much. She wanted to leave, to go back to Midian and I couldn't blame her. I knew right then that I had to do a better job of watching over her. Moses needed her and she needed him. For her to leave … well, it wouldn't help anyone and she would be more miserable than she was here.

"I took her under my wing then. I began spending more time with her, teaching her the languages, both Hebrew and Egyptian. We worked together and we grew close. She literally became the sister I never had the privilege of having and I adored her.

"As time passed and the things between Moses and Pharaoh became more intense, he withdrew into himself. He spent more time in prayer and talking to Aaron and not so much time with her. She resented that. Every woman would resent that. And, the fact that this God causing all of this trouble wasn't her god made it even more difficult for her. She didn't understand it all but she tried. I tried to help her understand it but there were times when we just couldn't span the language and cultural gulf between us. We tried. We laughed. We cried.

"That worked for a while but things became tenser and actually very dangerous. We all expected Pharaoh and his troops to ride in and wipe us all out. I don't know why he didn't. God, I guess. Anyway, Moses was worried about his family as well as the rest of us. Zipporah was a nervous wreck so he decided to send her back to Midian to her father, for the time being. He said she should go and then once we had left Egypt he would send word to her. She and the boys could join us then. It was an odd thing to do but I think he was as overwhelmed as she was. It really was a very dangerous time. By now, Moses was being forced to work alongside the men in some of the nastier jobs. It wasn't good. He wasn't sure he could protect her or his sons.

"She wasn't helpless, far from it. She was still new to our culture, to Egypt and to all that was happening. It had been hard going for her coming to Egypt in the first place and now an entire people were moving out. It was too much. She didn't want to leave him and go back to Midian but she didn't want to be here either. The decision was made, she would leave us for the time being, until things settled down. I helped her pack. Then Moses met his father-in-law at the Nile and sent her back with him.

"That caused a lot of problems, too. Everyone was mad that she got to escape the trouble and they had to stay, but Moses reassured them it was a temporary move. I hoped it was.

"When the night we were to leave finally came, I wanted us to all be together but Moses said he needed to be in his home in case anything happened. He needed to be where everyone knew how to reach him. It made sense. *Saba* Caleb and I took our family, your *ema* and *Dohd* Hur and our belongings and went to his house. Whatever happened, we were in this together.

"So we left. We started out and marched toward Yom Suph. No one knew for sure where we were going, I'm not sure Moses even knew. But we followed the cloud by day and the pillar of fire by night and we were safe. Probably for the first time in several generations we felt protected. And we had an angel of God traveling with us, Metatron, a true, live, visible angel. He looked like us but we knew who He was. It was a good feeling, for a while.

"When the crossing of the sea came we were all terrified. We were terrified of Pharaoh behind us and the walls of water on either side of us. It took a lot of faith to step into that channel that God had made for us. And, you have to remember, this was our God. I don't know how Zipporah would have handled it but I wished she was there to see it all. Moses was busy being Moses, directing the people, holding the staff up where everyone could see it. He had to focus on the people so it was probably good that she wasn't there.

"We made it through. All of us made it through. Not one person died or was lost. It was good and the celebration was great. We danced and danced until we didn't have another spin or turn in us. We were exhausted. The excitement was genuine and we had given it our all. We collapsed on the sandy beach laughing and crying. We women hugged then we sat and stared at the waves in the water for a long, long time.

"That night our families - that of Moses, Aaron and mine - all camped together. It was almost like a family reunion. It was the first time we had been able to stop and relax since Moses came back. We made a fire and sat around it, quietly retelling everything that had happened over the past six months after Moses and Zipporah came back to Egypt. I missed her and wished she had of stayed with us. She would have loved seeing the leaving.

"That time of relaxing and peace didn't last long. Early the next morning Moses and Aaron were up and organizing everything. We had to get ready to move on but we didn't know how all of that was going to happen. Moses seemed to have a plan. He called the tribal leaders together and they talked for hours. It was decided that we would move forward, toward the wilderness, in three days. Each leader had his instructions to get his tribe organized and we began putting our plans together and worked on organizing our families for the journey. We had no idea the journey would be so long.

"It was hard to get the people to stop and listen. Everyone had their own idea of how things should go, right down to the marching order and which tribe should lead. It was chaotic. There were intense arguments. Tempers flared. People stormed away from the meetings only to return later with sheepish looks on their faces and apologies. It was a hard time.

"We were on the journey for several weeks when one day Jethro showed up with Zipporah and the boys. I cannot tell you how excited I was. I had really missed her. She was probably the closest friend I had ever had, the only one that I felt I could totally trust. It was good.

"Jethro stayed for several weeks. He saw what all was going on and he was concerned. He knew the load Moses was carrying was huge and he was worried about it. He helped Moses see the necessity of setting up a judiciary system with the different levels of leadership. It was a great idea and Moses took it on right away. It took a couple of weeks to get it completely organized but you could see the relief on Moses' face. Soon thereafter, Jethro returned to Midian but not before he recognized and openly declared that our God, the One True God, is greater than all gods. Accompanied by Aaron, he offered a sacrifice, a burnt offering, to our God. It was such a sweet and good time and a blessing for Moses to know that his father-in-law, whom he had come to love and respect, now recognized our God as God! He returned to Midian and to his people, but he was a changed man.

"Zipporah and the boys stayed and we were so happy. Moses was happy too, but he was very busy and he didn't have much time for them. From that time on, Zipporah stayed close to us. She felt comfortable with us since Moses didn't really have time to be with her. In fact, he was gone a great deal of the time talking with God.

"We moved forward from there. Our communication skills became better, Zipporah's and mine, and she began telling me about her father, her home and all she had left behind. You could see that she still longed to go back but at the same time she was happy to be here with us. I believed I had to keep her with us, for Moses sake but maybe for mine as well.

"The first time Moses went up on the mountain, she was terrified. First of all, none of us knew he would be up there that long. We watched him go up and disappear into the cloud. A red hot glow settled on the top of the mountain, like a fire. We watched and we were terrified. Instructions had been given that no one was to set foot on the mountain so we couldn't send anyone up to see what was happening. We stood there for a long time, watching and waiting, thinking it wouldn't be long. It began to get dark and cold and we had to return to our tents.

"That night Zipporah and the boys came to our tent. They ended up staying with us the rest of the time he was on the mountain. She walked through her days in a trance. We all watched the mountain not knowing what was happening. We were frightened. We didn't know what to do. Aaron didn't hear anything from God nor did I. I don't know how many times I went off by myself asking to hear, praying for a sign, waiting. There was nothing. I did have the witness in my spirit that Moses was alive and well, but that was all. The red hot glow remained on the mountain and there was no sign of him.

"The people went crazy. They were scared. It appeared we had lost our leader. Some of the Egyptians that had come out with us went to Aaron and asked him to make an idol. They were so hyped up that they were threatening a return to Egypt. He argued with them but it didn't do any good. He really didn't care if they returned to Egypt, they were Egyptians, but he knew they'd pull some of our people along with them. He didn't want that. Things only got worse. Finally, he relented. He said he would make them an idol. It was a dumb thing to do but he didn't know what else to do. It was either that or a full blown rebellion.

"The people brought their gold to him and he began forming the idol. His wife, Dohdh Elisheba, was very upset with him. She knew it was wrong but she was also afraid they might kill Aaron if he didn't do something. She came to our tent and stayed with us. She and I prayed. Zipporah walked the floor, watching the top of the mountain and worrying. She told us she thought making an idol was wrong and that when and if Moses came back down the mountain he would be upset.

"I could tell she still wanted to leave. She didn't want to leave alone. I think she was hoping that when Moses did come down from the mountain and saw what had happened he would throw up his hands and leave. They could go back to Midian and live happily ever after. That didn't happen."

"No, I know it didn't. I've heard the stories about when he did come down and how he broke the stones, was angry, ground up the golden calf idol and made everyone drink from it. That was weird." Sarah said, remembering the stories she had heard as a small child. None of it had made sense to her then and it didn't now.

"Yes, it was weird but that's pretty much what happened. Moses wasn't just mad, he was furious. He struck out against the leaders of the rebellion and banished some of them. He did grind up the idol and pour it into the water. They had to drink of it. I'm not sure why he had them do that but he did.

"He didn't return to his tent like Zipporah wanted him to. Instead, he and Aaron went off and prayed. They sought the face of God, laying prostrate on the ground. The camp was quiet, very quiet. Everyone moved cautiously having come to their senses and realized what a sin they had committed. I think they were eager for instruction but also terrified of what that instruction might be.

"Zipporah said when Moses did come home, he was only there long enough to eat something then go back to prayer. Even those moments were rare. She said one day she heard him pounding on something. She stepped outside of their tent to see what was happening. He was building a box. She asked about it but he would only say God told him to build it. Later we learned it was for the broken stones that he had smashed to the ground when he came down and saw the bedlam that had ensued.

"The prayers and intercession he and Aaron made continued for forty days. She said she felt completely alone during that time. He was hardly talking to her. He wasn't mad at her but he was distracted. She felt like she had been replaced in his life by this Hebrew God and she didn't know what to do. She said she couldn't compete with this kind of love and she wanted to leave. Again, I talked her out of it. Maybe I should have let her go, for a time at least. But I didn't want her to leave and truthfully, neither did Moses.

"Then he went back up on the mountain. This time, everyone was really frightened. Moses told us that God had wanted to destroy all of us and start over but he argued with Him and got Him to change his mind. He said he wouldn't stand in the way if that happened again and we understood him, loud and clear."

"So how did that get you into trouble? I don't get it."

"That wasn't the problem. Zipporah was the problem. Or better yet, I should say my love of her was the problem. As I told you, when I first met her I loved her. Over the years our sisterhood grew and we became very close. She would confide in me and I in her. It was great. We knew we could trust her.

"But, I couldn't leave it there. Moses was off with God and Zipporah was having a hard time. I found Aaron and asked him to talk to Moses. He wanted to know why. What was up? I told him about Zipporah being so down because Moses was never around. I asked him if he didn't think he and I could take on some of the responsibility. We were all from the same family and we all had similar callings. Mine was prophecy. Aaron's was the priesthood. Moses was called to lead us out of all that we got ourselves into. I talked to Aaron at length until he finally agreed to talk to Moses with me. I thought if the two of us went together, a united front kind of thing that he might listen to us. That's what got me into trouble!"

"You got into trouble with Moses? That's what caused you to have tzara'at?"

"No. Not Moses. God." Miriam paused for a moment. She reached for her tea and took a long, slow drink. She sat the cup down and did a body shiver. Remembering this was particularly painful and she needed to pull herself together to be able to tell her granddaughter what had happened.

"I thought I was doing a good deed. Or at least, I told myself I thought I was doing a good thing. But my heart wasn't right. I was mad. I was right down mad at Moses for ignoring his wife. It wasn't right. I felt like he was doing the same thing our parents had done a generation before. By pulling away from each other and not sharing in the conjugal bliss of marriage that he was denying all that God had told us to do back when He had first called Abraham out. At least that is what I told myself I thought.

"Obviously, God knew that wasn't the truth." Her face paled a little as she remembered what happened. "I thought my argument was noble when I started out telling Moses, 'God has called all of us. Do you think you are more important than Aaron or me? Don't you know we can help you direct these people, lead them. You need to share the burden with us so you can spend time at home with your family. Aaron and I are just as important and capable as you are.' It all sounded good, or so I thought."

"What happened?"

"What happened? God happened! He told Moses that all three of us were to enter into the Tabernacle. I was excited. I thought we were going to get this straightened out for sure. And, that's what happened!

"We stepped into the Tabernacle and immediately a cloud came down and blocked the doorway and covered us. Then God spoke, audibly, to all three of us. He wasn't happy with Aaron and me but especially me. He said, 'Listen to My words. You are only a prophet. And, you are only a prophet because I appointed you to be one. I speak to you in visions and dreams only.' Now I knew He was speaking directly to me. Aaron wasn't a prophet, neither was Moses. Only me. My knees began shaking and I fell to the ground. Tears were flowing. I knew I was in trouble, big trouble!

"God continued, 'Moses isn't a prophet. I don't speak to him in dreams. He is faithful in everything I tell Him to do – in all My ways. I speak to him openly not in the darkness of night. He sees me and he knows me. Do you not understand that he is far more important in My work than you? Do you not understand that you have no right to speak against him? To speak against Moses is to speak against Me!'"

"Oh my gosh! I'm scared just hearing the story now. How did you feel? Was your heart broken?"

"How did I feel? I was terrified. I was humiliated. I was embarrassed. I had told myself what I was doing was good and because of my love for Zipporah. That was just an excuse. I was full of what I thought was righteous indignation, but it wasn't righteous. I was mad. I was judgmental and I was sticking my nose into something that wasn't any of my business."

Miriam grew silent. This was a hard memory. Her body tensed. The emotional heaviness of her experience was in her voice. She cleared her throat and continued with the story.

"Even telling the story to you now is very hard. I cannot tell you how terrified I was. The cloud lifted. When I looked down and saw my hands had turned white I screamed. They were as white as snow and as cold as a river on a winter's day. I could hardly move them. Then my feet began turning white and I felt the disease crawl up my legs like a choking snake that was squeezing the life blood from me. I screamed. I said I was sorry. I begged forgiveness. I fell face-forward on to the floor of the Tabernacle. I cried and cried, begging for mercy.

"Moses and Aaron were shocked. Aaron stood there trembling thinking he was next, but he immediately appealed to Moses on my behalf asking that this sin – our sin – not be held against me and that I not be counted among the dead with my flesh half eaten away." Miriam paused. A shadow of fear crossed her brow. Her eyes were wide and echoed terror as she remembered the tzara'at. "It really was terrible, for both of us.

"Moses shook himself out of the shock of seeing me like that. He heard the pleas of Aaron which I think was probably what was in his heart as well. He cried out to God to heal me. God's response was frightening as well as interesting.

"He said, 'If her father had spit in her face she would have to bear the shame of that for a week, for seven days.' Then He said, 'Let her be sealed outside of the camp for seven days then she'll be restored.'"

"What was that like for you? Not only did you have the *tzara'at* but you were banished to staying outside of the camp. What did you do?"

"I didn't have a choice. I was led out. I could hardly walk because of the *tzara'at*. My face was pale, marked by streaks of tears. No one touched me. They only stared, their mouths dropped open at the sight. I was led out by Aaron. He didn't say a word. He was upset and afraid, just as I was. I'm sure he was wondering what was going to happen to him. He was as nice to me as he could possibly be but he didn't look at me. He didn't hug me. He just pulled the tent flap up and motioned for me to go inside, then he lowered the side back down.

"I couldn't do anything. I couldn't use my hands. They were cold, stiff and totally numb. I watched to see if my fingers were going to fall off. Thankfully, they didn't. I was in shock. I couldn't think. I couldn't speak which was probably a good thing as that is what got me into trouble anyway – speaking. I sat down on a blanket on the dirt floor and stared at nothing. Then I cried again. I began praying and asking God to forgive me, begging for forgiveness, reminding him that I had a family to take care of. I couldn't eat. I didn't want to eat. I just prayed and cried. And I determined that I would never enter into gossip or manipulation again. What ever happened with Moses and his family was none of my business, I would just love them as they were."

"Oh, Softa, I cannot imagine what that had to be like for you. To be so alone, so abandoned. So scared." Sarah hugged her grandmother again, lingering in her great compassion for the woman whom she loved so much.

"I wasn't really abandoned. It felt like it, but I wasn't. The girls brought me food and slipped it under the tent sides and talked to me through the tent but I couldn't see them. I told them to go away. If they got caught coming out to me then they could get into trouble too. I told them I didn't want the food, I just wanted to be left alone. It was embarrassing as well as devastating. You know what a people person I am, yet here I am away from everyone for a week. I worried about the mother's giving birth. I worried about my children and what was happening to them. Granted, they were grown but I still worried about them. I worried about you, as little as you were then. And I worried about *Saba* Caleb. I missed him so much. I needed his comfort but he wasn't allowed to come to me."

"What happened? How did you know when to come out?"

"On the *erv* of the eighth day, Aaron came for me. He announced himself then he rolled up the tent side, just as he had done when he ushered me into the tent. I wondered what he was thinking but I am sure he had a great deal of guilt since he was involved in my rebellion as well."

"Yes. What about that? Aaron was involved in this but nothing happened to him, just the same as nothing happened to him over the golden calf but he was the one that made it. How did he escape the judgment?"

"I'm not sure. Neither he nor Moses ever explained it to me and I certainly wasn't going to question it after what had just happened. I don't know if it is because he is the High Priest, or his priestly garments or what it is, but I refused to ask. We are instructed not to touch God's anointed ones, so I didn't."

"Yes, but we are also instructed not to touch His prophets either. You were touched."

"True. I was touched but it was by God, not man. That is a huge difference. God can do whatever He wants to do or whatever He deems necessary. We don't have that right. We need to act responsibly, walk in the calling He places on our lives and stay out of other people's business. Believe me, I learned that one the hard way.

"I think this is one of the hardest things for any of us to learn, not to get caught up in the doings of other people, in their offenses. Often times some of the ladies would come to me and want to tell me their troubles. I would listen to their story and then I would ask them to pray and we would do that, pray and ask God to fix the situation. But I never got caught up in speaking against anyone again, that's *lashon hara* and I won't go there with them. If at all possible, I tried to send them to one of the Levitical priests after all of that was set up but I never went to the priest or anyone else to talk about the problems of others. It's a hard one but we can keep our mouths shut if we just talk to God and no one else. It can be done."

"How was Moses toward you after that?"

"He was good. You have to understand that Moses is a different kind of person. He walks in a level that we don't know or understand. He is so close to God that he really doesn't need people, yet he loves all of us so much that there have been several times that he has actually stood between God and God's destruction of all of us for our own foolishness. He is a true *tzaddik*.

"I never felt like Moses judged me for what I did, the *lashon hara*. I felt like he understood. He didn't agree with me but he understood. I'm sure my actions were small to him but he yields to God so he does what he is instructed to do. Remember, he interceded for me when all of that happened. Had he not done so, I probably would have died then.

"Another incredible thing that happened when I was banished from the camps and sent outside for those seven days, was the way the people stood with me. Normally they were a rowdy bunch wanting to move on and get to the Promised Land, but in this situation they just quietly waited. Maybe everyone was thinking this could have been them. I don't know. I do know they have always loved me and they respect me for the prophecy and the rock. But maybe it was just out of the kindness of their hearts.

"The good thing is that when I came out of the tent the *tzara'at* dropped off. It was gone and I was healed."

"I remember some of that, Softa. I know I was small at the time but I remember *Ema* being afraid and crying a lot. I didn't know why she was crying and no one ever explained all of that to me. Now I understand why she was so scared." Sarah moved closer to her grandmother and hugged her again.

"I know it was hard on everyone. *Dohd* Hur, your abba, said it about took him, our son, down. There is a bond between a man and his mother that is hard to break. He said when he learned what happened, he was angry and needed to get away. I asked him what he did to get away since we were so limited in where we could go while on this journey. He said he walked out into the desert looking for wood for the fires. He needed to be able to work off his frustrations. He said he, too, had a lot of questions about why the judgment didn't fall on his *Dohd* Aaron but he knew he had to let it go.

"When I did get to come out of the tent and back into the community, I felt humiliated. I knew everyone knew what had happened. I wanted to go back to our tent and just stay there but people were so kind. The women came and hugged me. They told me of the women who had delivered babies that week and what all had happened. I wouldn't let them gossip – I'd had enough of that. I think they'd learned too.

"A couple of days later we packed up and moved on to Paran and away from Hazeroth. I was relieved. There is always something about moving on that is healthy. For me, getting away from that spot was a good thing. There were too many terrifying memories of it all. I needed to look ahead."

"What about The Light? Did he not come to comfort you during this time?"

"No, He didn't. My isolation came from God and it meant that no one could come to me. In the aloneness I began to see myself as things really were. I wasn't quite as important as I thought I was. Yes, I am a prophet but even prophets can make mistakes. I learned that one pretty quickly that week. But, let's move on. I don't want to spend any more time dwelling on this. Time is short as it is."

Ten— Spies

"It was while we were in the wilderness of Paran that Moses sent the spies into Canaan. We had been traveling for nine months. We were tired yet very excited at the possibility of soon being home! Moses knew we would be facing armies so he thought we needed to know more about those people and what to expect. That was why he wanted to send in the spies. Of course, your Saba, as a leader of the tribe of Judah, was one of them chosen to go. I knew it before he ever told me and I knew he would come back, just as he did."

"How did you know? Did The Light come to you and tell you? How does that happen for you? The knowing?"

"No. The Light didn't come and tell me. It was the witness of the prophet within me I guess. You know, we have the gift of discernment and also intuition, if that's what you want to call it. Anyway, I knew your *Saba* Caleb would go.

"He came in, rather reluctantly at first, to tell me he was going. I think he thought I would be upset but I wasn't. This was important. We all knew, at least the family knew, that God would take us into Canaan and fight the battles for us as He promised. Moses wanted us to understand the enemy so we wouldn't run in fear. He wanted to know about the people that were living in Canaan. It was about being prepared."

"Why did he need to know that if he knew God would fight the battle for us?"

"I think he wanted to know what to warn the people about so they wouldn't be afraid and turn in the other direction, back toward Egypt. We were still an easily spooked bunch of people. Remember, we hadn't been gone from Egypt all that long. All of this happened the first year we were out of bondage. The people were still longing for the life they knew in Egypt, as hard as it was. This life, our new life, was one of uncertainty. It was full of promises but we had a long way to go before we were the people God wanted us to be. We were roughly hewn at that point.

"Moses sent the spies out, one from each tribe, with the instruction that they should go spy out the land and come back with a report. He wanted to know about the people of the land, what they were like. Were they warriors. He wanted to know about the cities. Were they open cities or were they fortified. Was the land good and plentiful? That's basically all he wanted to know. Remember, he had never been there either.

"So they went. All twelve of them. The night before they left there was a lot of celebration in the camp. We gathered together by tribes and celebrated with food and dance."

"Food? Weren't we already eating manna by then? What other foods did you have?"

"That's so funny. Of course we had manna. That's almost all we had, that and goat's milk. But our women are good cooks and they had experimented with the manna and had come up with all kinds of recipes. Some of them were pretty good. Occasionally the men would come in with something from the desert that could be used as a seasoning, but mostly we had a few herbs and a lot of ideas some of which were tasty, some not so much. But it was fun that night and we needed the release that it brought.

"We danced and sang. It was fun to do that, too. That was the largest celebration we'd had since we stood on the banks of the Yom Suph so it was very special."

"When did they leave?"'

"Early the next morning. I think Moses wanted them just to slip out of the camp but we didn't do it that way. We formed a couple of lines and they walked through them. Shofars blew and there was rejoicing. I think it was our way of overcoming the fear that we all had that maybe they were walking into danger and something might happen to them. Remember, these weren't just leaders of the tribes, these were our husbands, our fathers, our friends. We wanted them back."

"What happened? Do you know why they came back with such a bad report? I know that got us into a lot of trouble."

"Yes, it did. All I know is what your *Saba* Caleb told me. He said they went out as a group, the twelve of them sticking together. When they got to the borders of the Promised Land they argued about where they should go and how they should go about getting there. *Saba* and Joshua wanted to go first to Mach Pelah to pray and ask our forefathers for guidance and protection. The others didn't want to go there. They thought it was a waste of time so they separated and went their own way."

"Why did *Saba* and Joshua want to do that? Isn't Mach Pelah where Abraham and Sarah, Isaac and Rebekah and Jacob and Leah are buried? It's a cave, isn't it?"

"Yes, it is a cave and it is where they are buried. We see them as righteous people as well as our matriarchs and patriarchs. We believe, because of their righteousness, that when we go to where they are buried and pay tribute that they will ask for guidance for us and protection. It's just something that we do."

"If they are dead, how can they provide guidance and protection?"

"I guess that was the question the other ten men had as they refused to go there, saying it was a waste of time. *Saba* and Joshua didn't see it that way. They felt it was the right thing to do so that's what they did. *Saba* said after they had gone there and prayed they knew which direction they should go and what they should look for. It worked for them. When they came back they were laden with gifts for all of us. Gifts of fresh fruit from the Promised Land. It was amazing."

"Yes, I know. I remember hearing about that. Grapes. Huge grapes."

"Yes, it was a huge bunch of grapes, so large that they had to carry them back on a pole stretched between the two men. They gathered several large clusters in order to have enough to share around. But they also brought pomegranates and figs as well. With that, we understood that it truly was going to be the land of plenty. And that is our promise. Our hope. A land of plenty."

"So what happened then? How was it that we got into so much trouble with God?"

"Stupidity. Fear. Lack of faith. Maybe even laziness. I'm not sure. *Saba* said that when they were at Mach Pelah praying, they received an assuredness within their spirits that the land was ready for us and that all we had to do was move forward and it would be ours."

"But that didn't happen."

"No, it didn't happen. The other guys came back with a terrifying report. They told of giants in the land. Giants twice their size that made us look like grass hoppers. They were obviously frightened and their fear jumped off onto those in the camp and the people refused to move forward. They were crying. Threatening Moses. It was pretty bad.

"*Saba* spoke up, trying to quiet the people, to reassure them. He said, 'By all means, we should go in now and take the land. We can do it.' But the other ten. They made a much louder noise, telling the people all the reasons we couldn't do it. It was quite a scene. The people chose to believe the bad report. They said they were afraid that if we went into the land the people would murder us. It was pathetic. They had no faith, no trust. They just wanted it to be an easy situation. They were willing to trade the 'what if's' for the maltreatment that would be theirs if they returned to Egypt. They didn't take into consideration that our leaving Egypt had been at a great price to the Egyptians and returning there would be a death sentence to almost all of the adult males, out of revenge if nothing else!

"It was a mess, actually. The people cried and carried on. They accused Moses and Aaron of horrible things. Some of them even refused to speak to me. They refused to move ahead. They wanted to go back to Egypt. They even wanted to appoint a new leader for themselves to help them return to Egypt. It was chaos.

"That didn't happen. What did happen was God's anger. Both Moses and Aaron fell on their faces right there, in front of the entire congregation. They were pleading with God not to wipe out the people. This wasn't the first time they had rebelled and Moses felt He would just strike them dead.

"*Saba* and Joshua tried to reason with the people. They tore their clothing in agony and grief. It didn't do any good. They reassured the people that we could do this. They told our people

96

that the inhabitants of Canaan were our prey, that their protection had been removed from them. They wouldn't listen. Instead they were screaming "Stone them! Stone them!" It was very scary. You would think that after what had happened to me they would learn, but they didn't.

"As usual, they pushed too far and too hard. Then the glory of the Lord showed up in the Tabernacle. Everyone saw it. It was both terrifying and exciting. He was mad. He and Moses argued. God wanted Moses to step aside so He could destroy the people. Moses refused, arguing that if God did destroy the people then the Egyptians would hear of it. Not only would they rejoice but they would be assured that the only reason God had taken them out of Egypt was to destroy them. They would think their gods were the righteous ones. It was a mess.

"God wanted to start over with Moses. He wanted to destroy us and start over promising to make Moses a mighty people. But Moses didn't want that. I don't know why. Perhaps he had fought so long and so hard for us, suffered so much because of us, that he just couldn't give it up at this point. He kept saying no. But not just no! He argued with God, taking his own life in his hands. It was amazing."

"How do you know? Were you there in the Tabernacle?"

"No. No one was in there but Moses and Aaron, and God, of course. I heard some of it through the tent. I wasn't supposed to be that close but when I saw Moses and Aaron fall on their faces I ran forward thinking something had happened to my brothers. When I got to the door of the Tabernacle I saw that they were lying prostrate praying. I was frozen there. My breath was frozen within me. Panicked, I guess you could say.

"It was quite the debate. Moses was pleading for our very lives. He recounted to God how many times He had actually been seen, His power that is, by the Egyptians. He reminded God of the cloud of glory that was visible to all, the pillar of fire by night. He told God that if he slayed the people then Egypt would say they had won. They would believe that God couldn't control the Hebrews so He killed them and that would justify Egypt's treatment of us.

"Moses reminded God that He, God, was slow to anger and abundant in lovingkindness, forgiving iniquity and transgression. He said he knew the people were guilty and that the best thing God could do would be to let them live and pass judgment for their sin on to the next generations. He constantly was asking God for His forgiveness of the people, reminding God of His greatness and what the Egyptians would say if He killed us."

Miriam stopped for a moment. She stood and walked across the tent, pulling back the flap to allow fresh air in. She took a deep breath and then turned back toward Sarah to finish the telling.

"It was quite a battle there between God and Moses. Finally, God relented saying He would not destroy us. But none of us – that is none of us that were adults when we left Egypt – would see the Promised Land. Even though He had proven Himself to us again and again through amazing miracles, we still refused to believe or trust. Therefore, none of our generation – my generation – would be allowed to step foot into the Promised Land.

"That was a breath taking sentence. We would be kept out of the land. But, because He had promised not to kill us, you would have to wait to cross over into the Promised Land until we all died of natural causes. That was thirty-nine years ago and some of us are still alive. You still have to wait a while, my darling." Miriam told her cherished granddaughter. "You'll have to wait a few more months. We are so close. Perhaps that is why I'm leaving at this time. I'm part of that older generation and it's only fair that I leave now. In a way, it is setting you free to enter into the Promised Land. That will be so wonderful."

Sarah smiled a sad smile, nodding her understanding of what her grandmother had just told her. "How did the people take that?"

"Like they seemed to take everything Moses told them. Immediately they repented and said they were sorry. Then they said they would go, now, into the Promised Land. They wanted to move forward. But Moses told them "No!" He said, "Don't even think about it. It is too late. If you go up there now, after all that has happened, you'll be struck down in battle. The Lord is not with you." He went on to warn them that the Amalekites and Canaanites would be there waiting on them and they would be killed. As usual, they didn't listen to Moses and they charged ahead. "A lot of our people died that day. They were killed by the same enemy that just a few days before would have been annihilated by us. But the anointing on our people had been removed because of our rebellious nature. Basically, they killed themselves. Those who were not killed were badly injured. Some died of those injuries a few days later. It was sad. Very, very sad."

Eleven—Backwards

Miriam watched one ember then another as they escaped the fire and drifted toward the open tent flap, caught up in a haze of smoke and memories of days gone by. She turned toward her granddaughter.

"Things quieted down after that. There was a great deal to think about. People needed to look at themselves and make some decisions as to whether or not they were going to follow God and His instructions given through Moses or would they die in a state of rebellion. It was heavy. Much soul searching was going on.

"Even the children were quiet. I don't know if their parents were hushing them or if they felt the seriousness of the moment. But that's the way it was for several days after that. Quiet.

"Your parents came to our tent often during those days. You were just a baby. In fact, I think we all huddled together. We didn't know what to expect any more than anyone else.

"Slowly, things began to return to normal. Moses instructed us to be ready to leave as soon as the cloud departed. Once again, we were to follow it to wherever it led us which was actually a long day's journey back towards Egypt. The people were terrified. I think they thought God had decided to return them to Egypt as they had pleaded for. Instead, I think He was moving us back further away from the Promised Land now. It was spiritually out of our reach and I think He wanted it to be physically out of our reach as well.

"That was a hard journey for me. From a prophetic viewpoint, I knew and understood what He was doing. That didn't mean I liked it all that much. It was a step closer to that which I had left behind following the *tzara'at* and I didn't want any reminders. But maybe reminders was what we needed. Anyway, it was the location that the cloud took us to and where we settled for a while.

"God continued to get us organized here. He sat out some rules for us to follow. He sat out the rules for making animal sacrifices and required another sacrifice from us. It was like a parent that had severely corrected a bad child. Now He was trying to bring healing and a restoration of relationship to us. It was good that we had this opportunity to do something that would resemble acceptance of us by God and our acceptance of Him. The sacrifice brought healing.

"We had Egyptians with us when we left Egypt. Most of them were there with us by choice but some had been caught in the press of the moment and were afraid to go back. There were also the strangers, stragglers if you will, that had started following us in the journey. At first, I think they were staying at a distance, watching to see what God was going to do with us. After a while they began to realize that God was not going to kill us and, in fact, was protecting us in spite of ourselves.

"After a few weeks, they came into the camp and spoke to Aaron, Moses and Joshua, asking permission to join us. It was a challenge. We knew we were not supposed to intermarry with strangers, but here were these people who really wanted to unite with us and be a part of us. How were we to handle this?

"For a long time, several months I guess, they were allowed to come along but they had to stay apart from us, like an appendage. Then after all that had happened at the border of Canaan, it seemed that we needed the encouragement that we were good enough that people wanted to join themselves with us. I'm sure Moses and God had some conversations about this that we weren't aware of, but in the long run there were rules made for the sojourner that wanted to join with us.

"Moses called the leaders together and told them the rules. Then they instructed us. Basically, we were to treat the sojourners as one of ours and to do with them as we would want them to do with us. If we were required to sacrifice, then so were they. If they wished to sacrifice, then we were required to honor their request as long as it was to our God. No foreign gods or idols were allowed in the camp. It was simple and they became a part of us.

They became known as God-fearers and we accepted them in that light.

"Perhaps the most encouraging words from God that Moses relayed to us over the next couple of weeks was, 'when you come into the land where I bring you then you shall...'! That was exciting. It was as though a cloud of gloom had been lifted and we were being renewed in the hope that when the time was right we would be allowed to enter the Promised Land. It was a promise that we thought had been taken from us due to our actions. But, it hadn't been taken away. Delayed? Yes. But the day will come when we can enter the Promised Land. You'll be there, my dear Sarah. You'll raise your children in the Promised Land."

"I know. I'm happy about that. I'm so sad that you won't be there with us Softa. What ever will I do? You've always been here for me. I don't want to lose you."

"I know, my darling. I know. But this is okay. I'm going to my own Promised Land, one that is higher than the one you are going to. We will both be okay. You will always have the memories of our time together and they will bring you comfort, and even laughter. And, I'll be with my parents and those that have gone before me and we'll be waiting to welcome you when it's your time to come. But don't hurry it, okay. I want you to live and get to do the wonderful things that I've only dreamed of. They are yours to do."

The two women sat holding each other, both looking toward the future and the unknown.

After a prolonged moment, Sarah said, "Tell me more, Softa. Tell me everything you want me to know."

Miriam laughed. "Indeed, dear one. While we were there in that location we were renewed and refreshed with the idea that one day we would move forward. As I told you, rules were being established. I guess you could call it a form of government. We were trying to move from an unruly, rebellious people that was constantly in trouble with God to a people that honored and revered God. It was slow going at times.

"God wanted us to understand that the seventh day, the day of rest, was important. He showed us that with the manna when it first started falling. He set out the rules for collection. An *omer* a day per person for five days. On the sixth day we were supposed to collect double the amount so we could rest on the seventh day. He was strict about it. He called it the Sabbath and insisted we rest. No work was done. No one was out of their tent unless they were just milling around. We were limited in how far we could walk so we stayed pretty close to our own standards and banners and practiced obedience until the distance factor was settled.

"Then one day one of our people went out on the Sabbath to collect wood. I don't know why he did it on that day, but he did. When he was discovered by a couple of people out for a restful stroll, he was brought to Moses for judgment. Moses didn't know what to do with him as this had never happened before. He instructed that the man should be confined until he had time to ask Adonai what to do. The answer was pretty severe. The man was to be taken outside the camp and stoned to death! I guess we had to learn. It's like it was with my *tzara'at*, some things you just don't forget. No one was caught working on the seventh day, the Sabbath, after that.

"It was at that same time that the men were told they had to wear the tassels on the four corners of their garments, you know on the coverings they use when they pray. It was not only for setting us apart as a people unto Him but to remind ourselves that we are His and we need to walk accordingly."

"Yes, I know. We've started calling them *tallit* in our home."

"*Tallit*. That's cute. Simple. Who came up with that?"

"Yossi. You know he's always inventing something. Yossi started calling them *tallit* because he couldn't remember what they were called. He'd say, 'you know, *Ema*, the tell it thing.' Then it evolved from tell it to *tallit*."

"That's cute. I think that's what we ought to call the prayer shawl, the *Tallit*. I'm good with that." They both laughed, realizing that life is full of treasures, often times from the mouths of children. "The thing is, I know God was really trying to teach us that we are a people set apart for Him. It is important that we remember that. Why He would want us, I don't know. But He has chosen us and eventually, over the years, I think we began to understand that and walk in it. It has been good. I'm concerned for the future though."

"Why? What do you see happening in the future?"

"Without really strong leadership, I see our people getting caught up in cycles of rebellion and then repentance. It isn't just one time but over and over again. We must always have strong leaders. After Moses, there will be Joshua and he is strong. But after him, I don't know who it will be. God hasn't shown me and I haven't a clue. If that person isn't strong then we risk the chances of being destroyed, or back into captivity or scattered throughout the region with no home of our own.

"When I see things like that happening, I get frightened for the future of our people and I almost wish I hadn't been given the gift of prophecy. Sometimes it's almost a curse."

Twelve—Rebellion

"Out of everything that has happened, what was the worst or scariest thing that you've experienced? Was it the *tzara'at?*" Sarah asked.

"No, I don't think so. That was terribly frightening but I knew it was only for seven days. As terrible as that was, I understood there was an end to it and I would be okay again, even if I was humiliated. I think, for me, the scariest was Korah's rebellion. Do you remember any of that?"

"No, not really. I think what I remember is hearing my parents talk about it. They were very frightened."

"I'm sure. We all were or at least should have been. You know, you would think people would learn but we all seem to get in the way of ourselves. It messes up our thinking."

"Tell me that story? I don't remember it."

"Korah was a Levite you know, like our family. I guess he thought because he was a Levite and a member of the priestly tribe that he had special standing, and he did as far as being a Levite goes. But he wanted to be elevated to High Priest, which was Aaron's appointment. The truth was, no one but Moses had special standing and you would think my experience with the *tzara'at* would be proof of that. But I guess some of us need to be hit over the head personally. Korah was like that. He was a nice enough guy but he got caught up in some offense. I don't know if it started out as his offense or if it was someone else's but in the end, Korah was the one that squared off with Moses.

"It ended up, or by the time we were aware of it, it was two hundred and fifty people strong. Not all of them were Levites, some were from the tribe of Reuben, but the leaders were Korah, Dathan and Abiram. They confronted Moses and said, 'You've gone far enough. We are all holy, not just you. You act like you are the only one that is holy, that hears from God. Well, I tell you, we are tired of it. We are just as holy as you are. We are all chosen people. We all heard the voice of God that day, coming from the mountain, just as you did.'

"Actually, I could almost understand Korah's point of view. But, for Dathan and Abiram, not so much. The Tribe of Reuben, their tribe, didn't have any special standing because of the sins of their patriarch, Reuben, the son of Jacob. How they got involved in all of this, I never understood. What I did understand was this rebellion was dangerous, very dangerous. We were all still trying to figure out what it was that God had directed us to do so the timing was what was so treacherous.

"After it was all said and done, Moses and Aaron came to understand that Dathan and Abiram got pulled into the offense because they were neighbors of Korah."

"Neighbors? How can you mean that they were neighbors? I don't get that. They aren't of the same tribe."

"No. Not of the same tribe. But they were neighbors in the order of the way we were instructed to set up camp. Both of them, the Kohathites and the tribe of Reuben camped on the south side of the Tabernacle. As such, they were neighbors and probably became friends, or at least friendly, just because of the logistics of their assigned camps. When we pulled out to move to the next camping spot, they would have marched close to each other. That was all we could figure out.

"Korah, on the other hand, was a Kohathite, from the house of Kohath, our cousins. They were assigned tremendous responsibility for the holy things of the Tabernacle. Their job, once Aaron and his sons had taken down the holy utensils and covered them, including the Ark of the Covenant, was to carry them to the next location. It was a high honor and a lot of responsibility but the larger responsibility rested with Aaron, as High Priest, and his sons. It was Aaron and his sons that were the ones that covered the sacred items with the blue manatee fabric to get them ready to travel when the cloud lifted.

"Perhaps this is what made Korah so rebellious, knowing his family had the privilege of going into the Holy of Holies even if it was only to lift up the already packed items. Maybe that was what made them think they were as important as Aaron because it is only the High Priest that is allowed into the Holy of Holies.

"What they didn't take into consideration was once the items were taken down and packed, the Holy of Holies, as we normally think of that location, wasn't there anymore. It was with us, moving along with us, being a part of us. I'm not sure what happened, but something messed with their thinking. Maybe it was just jealously. I don't know. Again, where Dathan and Abiram fit into this, I never did understand other than the neighbor angle, but as I said, that understanding didn't come until later.

"Korah was pretty clever. He had managed to make cloaks for all of the two-hundred and fifty. Matching cloaks of blue, the same color of blue that Moses had told the men that they were to add a thread of to the corners of their *Tallits*. That was the first challenge. They said their 'clothing was already blue, so how could adding a single thread to the corner of it make any difference?' It was a challenge to the authority of Moses and the word of God.

"Moses was shocked. He had been so busy that he wasn't aware there was trouble brewing in the camp. None of us were. Neither Aaron nor I had been warned by God either through my prophetic dreams or he by the *Rauch HaKodesh*. Moses told them it was the command of God and they were to add the single thread of blue to the corner of their prayer shawls. Simple! It was an ordinance of God. They laughed! They told him how ridiculous it was to think a single thread of blue could make a difference since they were already completely clothed in blue.

"They went on to question Moses' authority in everything. In his so-called 'self-appointment' as the leader of us, but in the appointment of Aaron as High Priest as well. They told him that it wasn't just he and Aaron that had heard the voice of God on the mountain, we had all heard it. It was a very dangerous thing they were doing.

"Moses fell on his face before God, seeking wisdom. Then he told them, 'Okay. You've gone far enough with this. Tomorrow you come here, bring your bronze censers. All of you bring them. Tomorrow morning you'll put fire and incense in them in front of the Lord, and He will choose who is holy.

"This wasn't a test but a warning. It wasn't about whom God would choose as the High Priest. That had already been done. It was a warning to Korah to step down, to stop the challenge and to step back into his legitimate role as a Kohathite.

"Most people would have been scared to death. But, by now, Korah had puffed himself up a lot. He wanted a showdown and he was going to get it. The next morning, he did the last obedient thing he'd ever do. As instructed, he brought his censer to the gathering as did the men who had joined with him. Moses told them to put the fire in their censers and then the incense and God would choose the man who was holy.

"Personally, I would have stayed at home and hidden myself had I been in their shoes but they had gone so far they apparently felt they couldn't back down. Pride is a terrible thing. The odd thing though is that Dathan and Abiram, the men from Reuben, weren't with Korah and his buddies, for whatever reason. They refused to come.

"Moses sent a summons to them commanding them to come but they refused saying they didn't have to obey Moses. That only made it worse for them! Their venomous statement sent back to Moses didn't make any sense at all, at least not to anyone but them. But they still didn't come. The rest of them came, in their arrogance, with their censers in tow.

"Moses prayed to God and asked Him not to accept their offering as it was illicit. Once again, Aaron was confirmed as Priest and Moses was reaffirmed as the anointed leader."

"But how? God didn't rain fire down from heaven to destroy them, so what was the event that sealed it?"

"That's an interesting way to put that. Sealed it. That is exactly what did happen. Moses' prayer was that if these men, all two-hundred and fifty of them, lived their lives out and died a natural death then he, Moses, was to be judged as an illicit leader. Once again, God was angry. He told Moses and Aaron to separate themselves from this congregation, meaning all of us. He was going to rain fire and destruction down on us. But, Moses and Aaron interceded and God decided to punish only those who were involved in the plot.

"Then the Lord told Moses to tell all of us to stand away from the dwellings of Korah, Dathan and Abiram. Not only did he tell us to separate from them, but not to touch anything that was theirs or we would be swept away with the judgment for their sin. Even then, Korah, Dathan and Abiram stood in defiance. They and their families stood in front of the doorways of their tents almost challenging God to do something, so He did.

"While they were standing there, watching all that was happening, the earth opened up and swallowed them. Their wives, their children, their homes. All of them. There was nothing left of them when the earth closed up over them and sealed them in. And fire did come forth and consumed all of the two-hundred and fifty men offering up an illicit fire on their censers.

"It was then that it was made clear, very clear, that only the men of Levi were chosen to serve the Lord. It was frightening. Terribly frightening. But that wasn't enough. I guess the congregation got upset over the loss of Korah and his ilk plus the two-hundred and fifty, so they started murmuring about all that had happened. It was too much. God sent a plague upon us that was devastating. Within minutes thousands died. They were just falling over dead, without warning. Moses told Aaron to take the censer with fire on it from the altar, put incense on it and atone for the people. Aaron did that – he literally took the fire and ran amongst the people, standing between them and the death angel. Even so 14,700 people died that day. It was terrible."

"Did that stop the uprising?"

"Yes, for a while. Things were quiet. People repented. I think they began to reflect back on all that had happened. Perhaps they realized the price of rebellion was too high and they were the ones who had to pay it.

"It still puzzles me though. How can they do this knowing what happened to me as a result of my rebellion? I know Moses and Aaron love me as does Adonai and they know it too. You would think that having witnessed my mess, my judgment from the hands of God who loves me dearly, they would refrain from striking out at God's anointed but it didn't happen that way.

"But I think there was still some lingering discontent and confusion. People wanted the assurance that the three of us had not appointed ourselves to the rolls we were carrying out, especially that of the High Priest. In order to settle that once and for all, God instructed Moses on what to do. He told him to have the leader from each tribe to come to the Tabernacle, with their Tribal staff in hand. They were to write each man's name on his staff so there would be no argument about which staff belonged to whom. Later they told how over the years the wood in the staffs had become so hard that they could hardly carve their names in them, which made what happened to be even more of a miracle. Of course, Aaron represented our tribe, the Levitical tribe. Once they had followed the instructions Moses was to take all twelve of the staffs and place them in the Tent of Meeting in front of the testimony where God met and talked to Moses.

"God told Moses to tell the twelve men that the one whom God chooses to serve him will have his rod bud. Now if you think about it, that's a pretty awesome statement. A dead piece of wood that has been carried around by these guys for however long, would suddenly become alive. Not only that, it would bud. So that's what they did.

"The next morning, when they pulled the twelve staffs out of the Tabernacle. Aaron's rod had not only budded, it had bloomed and even produced almonds. After that there couldn't be any questioning as to who was God's chosen man. It was evident to everyone that another miracle had happened and it was Aaron that was chosen by God, not man.

"Things settled down after that. Who could argue with it? No magician, not even Moses, and I'm not saying he was a magician, could have made that happen. You know, it goes so much easier if we just quit struggling and accept God's will. I think the loss in the Korah rebellion, the loss of the two-hundred and fifty people and the plague would have been enough. But it wasn't. They didn't come to peace with things until the rod budded. That said it all."

Thirteen—Order

"Softa, I've never really understood how the camping order and the marching order came about. You referred to Korah and the tribe of Reuben being neighbors, but I don't get that either. Do you know how that all happened?"

"When we came out of Egypt there was a great deal of confusion on how we were to conduct ourselves. Although the Tribes were reestablished pretty quickly, there was still so much disorder and chaos. At first, we all just moved ahead, following the cloud without any form or definition. We were more like a huge mass of people, huddled together like a glob.

"That worked for a few weeks but it soon became obvious that we couldn't continue that way. It created too much animosity within the group. Everyone wanted to be first, to be the leader if you will, and that in itself caused problems. Sometimes we had to go through narrow passage ways due to tar pits or the like and it became dangerous with some of the people almost falling into them with the pushing and shoving that was going on.

"Finally, Moses had to do something about it in order to avoid complete mayhem. On one of his earlier trips up the mountain, Adonai began giving him instructions not only for the Tabernacle, but for how we were to camp and to move. When he came down and began to show us the plan, some of the people argued because they felt they were being mistreated by the order their tribes were placed in. But this was the command of Adonai and it had to be implemented.

"After all of the hollering died down the people finally decided to give it a try. They knew what we had been doing wasn't working and was only creating problems. Besides that they thought - we all thought - it was for just a few weeks since we would soon be entering into the promised land. As you know, that didn't happen. But, with God's plan, order began to be established.

"Although the Tabernacle had not yet been constructed God determined that it would always be the center of the camp. It had to be in a location where everyone could see it as well as the Shekinah glory that settled over it. And, the opening to the Tabernacle was always to face east."

"Why east? Why does that matter?"

"Because east of us, where we are now and where we came out of Egypt, is the land where God wrote His name. We are to face that spot, that location now and in the future. He wants us to see Him, know Him, commune with Him. In order to do that we need to direct our focus on Him.

"Once that was established, then we were to follow His instructions on how we were to set up camp. There would be times when we would have a lot of room and times when the camping areas would be small enough that we'd have to draw closer together. Because of that, there were two patterns, but the positions were always the same.

"As you know, the Levitical Tribe - our Tribe - won't have an inheritance when we enter the Promised Land like the other Tribes will have. Each of those Tribes will have a land inheritance which is set out by God, according to their size. We don't have that. What we have is the responsibility for the Tabernacle and its furnishings. That is our inheritance. Therefore, we are always to be close to the Tabernacle, surrounding it with our very presence until we finally reach the Promised Land. Then I believe we'll be scattered throughout the land so we can help others, but that won't happen for a long time, not until the land is cleared and the inheritances are established. For now, we are actually protecting the Tabernacle by being on three sides of it."

"Why just three sides? Why not all four?"

Miriam smiled. "That does create a lot of questions. I think it is because of our identification banner. You know our Tribes are identified by the color of the specific stone on the breastplate of the High Priest. We've all become connected with that color in one way or another, with most of us having the specific color somewhere on our tent to make it more easily identified. You know that. You have those two streamers on your tent by the opening. They identify your household as belong to the Levites.

"For us, the Levitical Tribe, our stone is the garnet which is a deep, dark red - almost blood red."

"Why do you think that is? Why would it be blood red?"

"The easy answer is because God said so. But the real reason, or at least what I think is the real reason, is because the priests deal in blood when they make the sacrifices. Our entire purpose is to certify the sacrificial animal, to offer the sacrifice along with the rituals that go with it and then to clean up from the sacrifice. It's all about the blood. By circling the Tabernacle on three sides, we are basically protecting it - in a symbolic way - with that blood. In essence we are walking out the meaning of the name of the Levitical Tribe which is *joined to God'*."

"What about the fourth side? Why does Judah always encamp in front of the Tabernacle, on the east side?"

"You know the answer to that without my telling you. But it is important that it get passed on correctly. It goes back generations, to our Matriarch Leah. When she named her children, those names had special meanings just as the names we give to our children today. Judah means *praise*. I believe Judah guards the entrance to the Tabernacle so that we, all of us, can come to understand that the only way into the presence of God is through praise. If we really want to know Him personally, like Moses does, then we have to be willing to dedicate our lives to praising and worshipping Him.

"By that same thought, almost every time the cloud moves and we march on, it is Judah that leads us. Occasionally, we take the lead but most of the time it is Judah. My thoughts on this are that when praise goes forth it clears the way for the rest of us to follow, just as Moses did years ago at the Yom Suph.

"Praise takes us into the presence of God but I believe it also invites the presence of God into our lives. Therefore, if praise goes before us then the way is much smoother. I think this is why we've won all of our battles so far. The presence of God can't be overcome except by sin. If we are not walking with Him, but walking in sin, then His presence will not move forward with us. At least that is my thought on all of it.

115

"Just as Judah leads us, so does Dan always bring up the rear or the tail, as we move forward. Dan is the second largest Tribe, next in count to Judah. Like Judah, the number of warriors he has is very large. By coming behind he is not only picking up the stragglers and things left behind, but he is providing a wall to keep out any would be attackers from the backside of our tribal community. His job is important. Actually, every Tribe has a specific job or purpose that is important in keeping us safe and carrying out the work of God. In the end, it all matters. No one is more important than anyone else. I think that is a hard one for people to understand and come to grips with.

"As to the relationship between Korah and the Reubenites, it happened because of the positioning, not only during our encampment but in moving out as well. Korah was camped on the south side of the Tabernacle. By the same token, Reuben, Gad and Simeon also camped on the south side. But it was Reuben, the leader of those three that was actually situated closer to Korah's family.

"I suppose they spent time together in fellowship, just like we've fellowshipped with other tribes. It is a natural thing to do. You and I both know that when you fellowship with people and really get to know them, they open up to you and begin sharing their thoughts and feelings. I think that's what happened here.

"Korah was a close relative of ours. He wanted to be High Priest. He wasn't interested in the fact that it was God that ordained Moses and Aaron. He wanted it to be a vote of the people and he was sure he could win the vote. That's probably why he was so interested in having everyone identify with him through the blue robes and all. I don't know that for sure, no one does. But as I've thought about it, that's what makes sense to me."

"You haven't been given any visions or interpretations about it?"

"No. Just my own thoughts on it. Usually it is jealousy that gets people into trouble. I think that's what it was with Korah. He was jealous. I'm sure he saw the respect the people have towards Aaron and Moses and he wanted that. He didn't understand that you can't legislate that, it has to come from the heart. Somehow he was able to get Dathan and Abiram to join in with him and to bring along their friends. That's usually how it happens. Jealousy can be contagious, you know. It works like a grain of sand in the belly of the oyster. It irritates and irritates. Unfortunately, nothing beautiful comes out of human jealousy. Only bitterness, resentment and eventually, devastation. That's what I think happened in this situation. Korah just couldn't leave it alone. Had he done so and repented before God, there is a chance he could have been more significant than he thought himself to be. It ended in tragedy. Jealously always does."

Fourteen—Remembering

"Softa, in all of this what was your favorite thing that happened. What made you the happiest?"

"Lots of things, I guess. Of course, the happiest times for me and for your *Saba* Caleb, were when you little ones were born. Grandchildren bring joy to our hearts and encouragement to us concerning the future. Every time God gave us a new grandchild we felt renewed and encouraged. For the first time in a very long time, we had hopes for our future and that of our people.

"But there were other times as well. I think the thing I loved the most was building the Tabernacle. It was a tremendous undertaking. There was so much to do and we had to do everything from the very beginning. We didn't just have to dye the fabric. We had to shear the sheep to get the wool then we had to spin the thread to make the fabric. Moses was intense on our following the directions specifically, no variance from what God had shown him when he was on the mountain. He told us which snails or flowers or plants would provide certain colors and how to obtain those dyes from them. That entire process was fascinating and, as you know, the colors turned out to be beautiful.

"There was joy in the work. I think all of us finally felt we were doing something for our God – the One True God. We were excited. We were honored. Men and women brought forth gold and fabric and supplies with smiles on their faces and some even with tears in their eyes, tears of joy that they were being allowed to participate out of love and not a demand. It was all volunteer. Each man and woman was to bring what their heart lead them to bring. In fact, it wasn't long before we had more supplies than what was needed and they had to tell the people to quit bringing items.

"We had been through a lot as a people. We had suffered and died together. We had sacrificed so much to the slavery of Egypt. Now we were free. We were establishing a government and we had our own God. A true, living God. We weren't being pressured to worship a silly statue of clay or iron made by the hands of man. We had a real, live, loving God and we were free to worship Him openly and honestly. It was so exciting.

"It was a lot of work but it was done with a cheerful heart. People sang songs of praise as they wove the fabric, died the wool, found the wood. It was a beautiful time of unity and oneness within our families. I loved it. Everyone loved it. We were preparing a place for God to dwell amongst us. It was a thrill.

"We all wanted to do it right. We had seen the fury of God when we had been disobedient. Now we wanted to see His love extended to us in a tangible way, over and above all of the miracles we had already experienced. I just loved that time. So did your parents. They were beginning their own families by then and they were excited to be a part of this coming together and realizing the fulfillment of the promises God had made to Abraham, Isaac and Jacob.

"I believe with the building of the Tabernacle came a deeper faith in God, a better understanding of who He is and what He wants and expects from us. I think it also renewed our faith that we really would enter into the Promised Land, the land of milk and honey. I still believe that. I know I'm not going to see it, but you will. You'll raise your little ones there and there will be great joy for all of you.

"Don't mistake me on this. I know entering into the Promised Land won't be all that easy as has already been proven by the wars we've had to fight along the way. I think back to the first war we had to fight, right after coming out of Egypt. We were still a rag tag bunch of misfits then, but God was with us then just as He is now.

"We had a make shift army though, be that as it may. We didn't have much in the form of weapons. Mostly it was what we had gathered from the Yom Suph after Pharaoh and his army drowned. We were able to salvage a few shields and lances, that type of thing but they were pretty scarce. Our guys hadn't been trained to do anything but physical labor but that work had made them strong. The one thing we had going for us was God and His placement of Moses on that high bluff overlooking the battlefield. That was amazing.

"We were just feeling our way, learning to walk with God when we were attacked by Amalek at Rephidim. It was a shock. We weren't prepared for war but it was pushed upon us. Moses told Joshua to choose men to take into battle with him and he, Moses, would stand on the hill and fight the battle from there, holding his staff high.

"As long as Moses' hands were lifted heavenward, Joshua and the men fighting the battle on our side were winning. When Moses' arms got tired and he couldn't hold them up any longer our side began to lose. Aaron and your *Dohd* Hur saw what was happening so they sat him on a boulder and held his hands up for him. It was a joint effort and we won. We should have learned a lot from that but I don't think we did other than we would have to do battle and we needed to get prepared. Mostly, we were just excited.

"After the battle, our men salvaged the weapons of the enemy that they left behind as they fled. We studied those designs and began to make our own weapons. That helped us build our military capacity. Joshua saw what all happened and he realized that we needed to get serious about forming a strong army for our own defense. He and Moses were very close and they worked together. They made a plan and Moses appointed Joshua as the general. He worked with the men, twenty years old and up, and trained our guys to be warriors. It apparently worked as we have won the rest of our wars up to this point. Some more easily than others, but we have never forgotten that we win because God is with us.

"It is my prayer that as you enter into the Promised Land you will continue to win the wars that you have to face. It won't be easy. God never promised us easy. He did promise us He would never leave or forsake us and that is pretty much the way it has been. I love the fact that He is with us, even now as I prepare to go on my final journey."

"I know, Softa, what you are saying is true. Not only do I remember a great deal of this but there is that witness within my spirit that God is, and has always been, with us. Sometimes I don't know how He stands us, but He does. What I wish is that He would allow you to stay with us as well, that you could go into the Promised Land with us."

"I know, Darling. I wish I could go in with you as well as it will be very exciting. But, God has His plans. A big part of that plan is that my generation, and that means all of us, have to die before you can cross over into the Promised Land. I know in my spirit that it won't be all that long before my brothers join me on the other side and I think that will be exciting as well. Maybe we can actually have a conversation for a change. Wouldn't that be fun? Can you imagine the three of us sitting around talking about everything that has happened?"

The two women fell silent as each dealt with her own emotions. Knowing that the final separation was coming soon was difficult for both of them. They each knew that life would go on, that the promises of God would be carried out and that Sarah and her family, as well as the rest of Israel would be just fine. That didn't make the emotions of the moment any easier.

"The Tabernacle, Softa. You were telling me about the Tabernacle and how it felt to make it when we got sidetracked. Would you finish that story?"

Miriam laughed. "I guess I still have challenges with getting sidetracked don't I. I just get to thinking about something that comes up in the telling that reminds me of something else and before you know it, I'm walking down that road.

"The Tabernacle was amazing. It took a while, maybe six months, to build it. As I said, everything had to be just so. Once we had completed making the curtains, the walls, the objects that were to help with the worship – you know, the lampstand, the brazen altar, the shewbread table, etc. – it all had to be assembled in a specific order.

"Once that was done, the priests had to be established and taught. That's where our family comes into the picture. It wasn't just Moses, Aaron and Me, it was our entire tribe. While not all of us are called into the leadership, we are all called to worship the Lord and to do His service in the Tabernacle. Some of us are singers so we praise the Lord. Some of us blow trumpets so we blow the silver trumpets and sound the shofar. All of us have specific tasks in addition to our duties of carrying the furnishings. It is an important job that isn't always with a lot of glory. In fact, there isn't a lot of glory to it. We take the work pretty seriously. Only the High Priest is allowed into the Holy of Holies and that's only once a year. The rest of the time, it is carrying out the blood sacrifices that are required by God. Sometimes it is pretty messy but over time and with practice the priests have learned how to do it all in an orderly manner.

"They are pretty serious about it all as it can be a life or death situation for them. Most of the time it is about working in a precise fashion. Breaking down the Tabernacle. Setting it back up. Carrying it in a specific order and being quick about it. We cannot really have an established encampment until the Tabernacle is set up each time. Then and only then does the Presence of the Lord return to us. It is important work although no one should get over impressed with themselves because of it. Sometimes I think it would have been easier if another tribe had been chosen to do that work, but for some reason God chose us."

"Why do you think He chose the Levites to be His servant tribe?"

"It certainly wasn't because of anything we did. I don't think we deserved it, especially if you go back to when our Patriarch Jacob brought our people into Canaan originally. It was Simeon and Levi that caused the sons of Shechem to be circumcised and then killed them all. That was pretty bad and it caused a lot of issues for a while. Perhaps it was because of the zeal that He chose us, but I think it was most likely because we were one of the smallest tribes. Anyway, this is our inheritance, serving the Lord God and worshipping Him. I'm honored to be a part of it and I'm thankful He chose our family, as hard as it gets sometimes."

Again, the women, grandmother and granddaughter, paused to think about all they had discussed. At times the discussion had been heavy and serious. At other times it had been easy and full of joy. But always, there was the knowing that this was the last time they would be together, whether The Light came today or in the night, time together was running out.

"As glorious and magnificent as the Tabernacle is, the day will come when our people, all of the tribes, will gather together to build a magnificent Temple on a mountain top where God's presence will come and abide amongst us. They will know the location several ways but definitely because He will have written His name on that spot. It is a long time from now but it will happen and it will be a sight to see. I can see it now. Large stones. Lots of white and gold. There will be special places for men and women to worship the Lord, apart from each other. It will be wonderful.

"The priests will sing songs of praise and those songs will echo throughout the hills of the land. It will be a holy experience, one that will cause men and women to come to this place, to the Temple to worship the One True God and all men will be glad. That will be a sight to see. I hope you get to see it, Sarah, but I have a feeling it is a long, long way off. But, it will happen."

Fifteen—Dedication

"You asked what one of my favorite things was. Maybe it was the week of dedication of the priests. That was fabulous. After the *Ohel Moed* – Tabernacle - was dedicated to the Lord, it was time to dedicate and establish the priestly line. Aaron and his sons were the ones to be ordained. Aaron, of course, was to be ordained as High Priest and the four sons, Nadab, Abihu, Eleazar and Itamar were to serve as priests. They all looked so beautiful that day.

"It wasn't a simple thing. There was a precise routine to be followed. Moses was leading and instructing. Although he wasn't a High Priest, he was the one with the direct communication with and to God and he was the only one that knew what the requirements would be.

"Everyone was assembled for the event. It was a huge crowd of people but it was being done in such a way that almost everyone could see what was happening. Aaron and his four sons were brought forth, along with their garments and the anointing oil. A bull was brought forward that would serve as the sacrifice for the sin offering. Two rams and a basket containing bread that was unleavened was also brought forward as part of the ceremony. We met at the *Ohel Moed* where all of this was to occur, but we weren't allowed inside. We could only watch from the outside.

"Moses brought all five of them forward, washed them with water and then started by putting Aaron's tunic on him first. When that was done he brought him to the door of the *Ohel Moed*, where we could see what was happening. In a very ceremonial way he tied the sash around Aaron's waist, then the robe, then he put the ephod on him. The ceremony was beautifully done in such a holy manner. The ephod was made of gold, blue, purple and red yarns. There was hammered gold, hammered very fine and shaped into threads to be woven amongst the yarn, thus strengthening it as well as making it even more elegant.

"The ephod was gloriously designed with a stone for each of the Twelve Tribes on the front, placed in order of the birth of the twelve sons of Jacob. The colors of those stones were beautifully radiant as they were attached to the breastplate – the ephod – with gold mountings crafted by those who had learned the skills in Egypt. There were the blues and greens and yellows and turquoise. You know. You've seen it every time Aaron puts it on. Don't you think it is magnificent?"

"Yes, I do. I always get spiritual chills when I see it. I know how very special it is."

"The ephod is connected at the shoulders with two beautiful black onyx stones that have the names of the twelve tribes engraved on them, six to each side. On the inside of the ephod, where no one could see it but we all knew it is there, is a pocket that holds the Urim and the Thummim which are used for casting lots and judgment. It is glorious. Then Moses placed the turban on Aaron's head along with the gold plate that he put over his forehead, just as the Lord had commanded him. It almost looks like a crown, but it isn't. It is a hat that determines servitude and says, 'Holy to the Lord' on it. What a statement.

"Aaron was anointed with oil, then the *Ohel Moed* was anointed with oil along with everything in it. Moses sprinkled the altar seven times with the anointing oil, but none of us could see that. We were told about it later. Everything was done with the explicit instructions of God. No man orchestrated what was to happen.

"After that, Aaron's four sons were called forward where Moses put the priestly garments on them, draped them with the same type of sashes along with specific head covers that we see the priest wear all the time.

"Then the bull was presented for a sin offering. Aaron and his sons had to put their hands on the head of the bull in a symbolic effort to transfer their sins to it. The blood was what was important. In order for sins to be forgiven it seems blood has to be shed. It is hard to realize that something has to die for us to be forgiven, but that's what God instructed and we were determined to follow His teaching.

"Blood was sprinkled on the altar and around the *Ohel Moed*, according to instructions then the burnt offering was made. As always, the burnt offering was completely consumed by fire in an extravagant symbol of absolute love for God. Normally, a portion of the offering is retained for the priests and for the ones making it, but in a burnt offering, it is entirely consumed.

"Then the ram was offered and the remaining ceremonial offerings were made. It was beautifully symbolic and left us all knowing something special had happened. After that, Aaron and his sons were to remain in the *Ohel Moed* for seven days before coming out. These were the days of their ordination, a time of setting apart unto the Lord. They were to remain at the entrance of the *Ohel Moed* with instructions to be ready to do what the Lord required of them. Had they not obeyed and gone in, beyond where they were supposed to be, I'm sure fire would have rained down from heaven and destroyed them.

"While it was all very exciting, it was also nerve wracking. This was a big part of our immediate family. If something happened to Aaron I knew I would be a mess. I prayed for them. I prayed they would be obedient, hear God and be precise in what they did with His instructions."

"Apparently it worked," said Sarah. "They survived the dedication and the week of being set apart and actually were functioning very well as priests then, weren't they? That is until Nadab and Abihu offered up the strange fire. That put a stop to any ideas the priest might have that were not of God. I've always wondered, why do you think God killed them for that fire?"

"They offered up a fire they weren't authorized to offer up. The thought is that they had been drinking and they got carried away with the priestly instructions. I don't know if that is true or not, but whatever they did, they obviously weren't obedient and God wasn't going to put up with that, especially in the *Ohel Moed*. He killed them!

"Nadab and Abihu had been part of the assembly of the seventy that God had called up to the mountain when He confirmed the Covenant with us as His people. He had been very specific in calling out Aaron and his four sons along with the seventy. Moses got up early that morning - the day that they were to go up on the mountain - and built an altar to the Lord. Then they all made blood sacrifices unto the Lord before they went up on the mountain where they actually saw the Lord, at least His feet. They told how under His feet was a beautiful pavement of Lapis Lazuli, as magnificent as the sky. They were very excited and humbled at having been allowed this privilege of going up with Moses and entering into the presence of the Lord.

"They saw God and they ate and drank with Him. He didn't destroy them or harm them. He fellowshipped with them, all seventy of them as well as Aaron's family. From there, Moses went on up the mountain to be with the Lord leaving Aaron and Hur in charge and sending the others back down. I can't help but think there was something in that encounter with God that made Nadab and Abihu think they had been given special privilege. I don't know. By getting ahead of God, not waiting on Him, we show a disrespect for Him that is unacceptable to Him. I do know that we should never run ahead of God or take Him for granted. He wants everything done in His time and in His way. I think they just got caught up in all that had happened and didn't stop to think. I guess we'll never know for sure why it happened like it did.

"The loss of them was hard for all of us, but especially Aaron. God told him he was not allowed to mourn them. He was to carry on with his priestly duties. He did that out of rote, I think. I know he was devastated yet God told him he couldn't grieve over them. After that, they were supposed to eat the remainder of the offering but they didn't do it, they burned it instead. When Moses confronted him about it his answer was understandable. He said 'it was for a sin offering and for him to have eaten it that day would have been a sin since he was in despair over the loss of his sons'. Moses understood and saw to it that nothing happened to Aaron over that infraction.

"Sometimes God is beautiful beyond imagination and at other times, His fury is such that anyone who survives should count themselves as fortunate and even favored. I know about God's fury, but most importantly, I know of His love which is so warm and beautiful that it overrides anything harsh that we've experienced from Him."

Sixteen—Finding Home

"Come on, let's walk," Miriam said, breaking the silence and heaviness over the thought of never seeing each other again. "It's a beautiful day. Let's take in the sunshine and the gorgeous desert scenery. It won't be long before neither of us is living on this desert so let's take it in and maybe even watch the beautiful sunset."

They walked for a short distance, taking in the exquisite ruggedness of the desert. In its almost blank canvas of blacks and whites and tans there was beauty if you looked hard enough to find it, and they did.

"Here, let's sit under this tree for a little while. We can sit in the shade and talk. It's early in the season yet but the mid-day sun is already hot. This acacia tree will provide a comfortable place to sit and watch everything that is going on in the camp." Miriam said, moving a small rock out of the way, taking care to make sure there were no deadly desert creatures under it. She raked her hand over the sand, smoothing it to make a comfortable sitting area.

The two women sat and remained quiet for a few minutes while each of them thought of the last few hours and all that had unfolded. So much history had been shared, so much emotion. What else was there to say, yet Sarah was afraid if her grandmother quit talking she would be taken. She didn't want that. She hated the thought of it.

"What was the most fun thing you remember?" Sarah asked, wishing to keep her grandmother talking forever.

"The most fun thing? Hmmmm." Miriam said, looking back through the memories stored in her mind. "I think the most fun thing was figuring out how to identify ourselves – our tents that is – to our children. When we came out of Egypt we didn't have much. We were a rag tag bunch of people, poorly organized and just rambling along from location to location. After a few weeks we began to realize that we couldn't remain so disorganized. Moses was constantly before God and then coming back with instructions. We had the choice of just sitting and waiting or starting to do things for ourselves. Aaron and some of the men decided that we needed to take count of our provisions for housing and figure out what to do. It was obvious that what we had was very temporary and entirely too sparse for such a large crowd of people. We were okay for the time being but we wouldn't last long without shelter.

"They began checking with each family and trying to keep track of what provisions they had. Was it a tent? Was it a blanket? What form of shelter did they have? Not only were the results all over the place but it was so unstable that it wasn't going to last more than a couple of weeks.

"Trying to account for each family got too cumbersome so they decided to divide up into groups. Moses came back from one of his meetings with God and said the groups should be by tribes then by families, then by smaller families. By this time there was some confusion as to who belonged to which tribe but through a serious effort of going back through family history and talking to the older people, we began to figure it all out.

"There were some issues that had to be dealt with though. One of those was in the case of a marriage of two people from different tribes. Which tribe did they belong to? It was decided that they would belong to the husband's tribe from then on. That was the simplest way to make it work.

"Once the tribal relationships were re-established, we had to figure out which tribe needed the most help. It turned out, it was pretty even." She smiled, remembering back over those days that seemed so long ago now. 'Could it really have been almost forty years,' she asked herself. She shook her head in awe of it all.

"What? What is it, Softa? What's wrong?" Sarah asked.

"Nothing is wrong. I was just remembering. It's funny, time passes so quickly that we forget about our own history. That's why it is so important that you remember what I'm telling you now. It must be remembered and passed down to your children and their children and their children. It is the history of our people. If we don't remember, if we don't pass it down, then one day it will all blow away just like the sand storms we've seen on this desert journey. We can't let that happen. Do you understand?"

"Yes, Softa, I do understand. I really do. I'll pass it on to my children and my grandchildren. I won't forget and I won't let them forget you."

"I'm not what is important. Our history is what is important."

Both women sat fighting tears, thinking of the future. Sarah was devastated that her beloved grandmother would be leaving her and wouldn't cross over into the Promised Land with them. She thought she had probably suspected that in recent months but now that it was here facing her, she didn't know what to do.

Miriam was remembering the journey to this point, along with the hardships and the joys. There was room for tears and there was room for laughter. It had all been one long, hard journey and now her portion of it was coming to an end. Her biggest reward, in all of it, sat here with her under the shade of the acacia tree.

Miriam broke the silence, continuing with the history of her people.

"They decided that the first thing that had to happen would be to make new tents. Of course, you know as well as I do, that meant shearing the goats, weaving the hair into the coarse threads to make the tents. Because there was no way we could have enough goat hair those first few years, we had to compromise by making one huge tent roof for each family and then using blankets or whatever we had for the sides.

"Wood for supports was hard to come by in the desert wilderness. We searched for wood that would be strong enough. Sometimes we got lucky and found fallen limbs from old trees that had washed up from flash flooding and were able to make several supports out of them. It was hard going at first. We used what we had. We made what we could. We learned to do without. It wasn't too bad. We were all in this together and we helped each other survive. Occasionally someone would pull away, trying to keep their belongings for themselves and that was okay. But generally, everyone shared as much as possible. Even those who pulled away seemed to come to their senses, repent and rejoin the survival effort after a few days.

"As I said, over time things got a little easier. The further away from Egypt we got the more willing we were to pull together. There wasn't that desire to go back to the easy life." She smiled again. "I guess that's up to anyone's definition of easy. I loved being away from Egypt. Being out here in the open spaces, looking forward to the Promised Land and all that it held for us. I could see it. Perhaps it was just because of my prophetic gifting that I could see it, but I know that one day our Promised Land will be magnificent and all nations will want to come to visit. That's a long way off though.

"After a couple of years we had a lot of black tents. And I do mean a lot! It was like a sea of tents that had little to distinguish one from another. That was a challenge. Every tent looked the same, especially to the children. There was a Council meeting about it and how we should go about solving the problem. By now, our camping order had been determined by God but it was still hard to recognize our specific tribe. It was decided that each tribe would have a banner, a flag of sorts, and that banner would represent their households.

"But that created another problem. How were they to decide on the color and the emblem? God decided for us. It was simple, really. In His instructions to Moses regarding the priestly garb, the ephod was included which held a different stone for each tribe. It was the color of that stone that would become the official color of the banner for each tribe."

"I'm glad you brought that up. How did we know to do some of these things? We had been slaves in Egypt building cities. Yet here we are just days, weeks, and months away from Egypt and we are making the ephod, carving stones and all of that. How did that happen? How did we know how to do that?"

"Believe it or not, we learned how to do everything we needed to survive in Egypt. It was almost like it had been a training ground for us. Not everyone was building the cities. Some of us were used in foundries where we learned about molting metal. Some of us were taught how to weave so we knew how to make cloth. Some of us worked in farming, in industry. All types of things. We were slaves so we weren't paid, but we were taught. We were expected to produce and produce well. Our products were of the highest quality. Our lives depended on it. The Egyptians thought nothing of beating us or killing us if we didn't do it right so we learned our various skills extremely well. They had no idea they were training us for the future. And we didn't either.

"You know the ephod of the High Priest that your *Dohd* Aaron wears, did you ever stop to think that the etching on those stones was because of what someone learned to do in Egypt? Not only that, the onyx ephods that he wears on his shoulders with the names of the tribes on them, that skill also came from Egypt. Little did they know that the skills we learned in their land would allow us the ability to always have the names of the twelve tribes before our God. That's what happens when the High Priest wears those epaulets on his shoulders, he is lifting us up before God, each tribe by name. It is like a reminder to God so He doesn't forget our name. It is amazing when you stop to think about it.

"When we came out of Egypt we had skills equal to those of fine workmen. We didn't always have the raw product but soon we figured out how to find that. Always, God provided. It was a miracle. Every day was a miracle. I know I keep saying that but you need to really understand that.

"An example of that was our goats. Not only did they multiply rapidly, but they provided an abundance of hair as well as goats milk. What little we started out with just kept growing and growing. It was always enough. Not only did our animals grow in number but so did our people. You would think with all of the plagues and punishments we suffered that we would have dwindled, but we didn't. God had said, 'be fruitful and multiply' and we were obedient to that one!"

Both women laughed at the absurdity of it all. Here they were, two women sitting under a tree in the desert talking about all that had been and the soon death of one of them and they were laughing. The more they thought of that, the more they laughed.

Miriam pulled Sarah closer to her, hugged her tight and held her for another lingering moment. It was good. They were good. They understood what had been and what was yet to be.

"But that wasn't all of it. Once we got the tent identification figured out, we had to have a pattern for setting up and moving out. God took care of that one as well. He set out a pattern for us to live by which included the order we were to move in when we followed the cloud to the next location and how we were to set up the encampment when we settled somewhere. We were learning. Always learning. Not only did we learn to make things in large quantities for the entire camp, but in smaller quantities for our own families.

"We began listening to God and Moses more. Moses would go before God and get instructions and then pass them on to us. When we followed them, things went pretty well. It was when we didn't follow them that things began falling apart."

"Softa, wait a minute. I want to go get something from my tent. Sit here and I'll hurry. Please don't go." Sarah looked at her grandmother hesitantly. She didn't know if she should leave or not. What if the The Light came while she was gone, then she would miss her grandmother's leaving. She wanted to be here. She didn't want to leave but she longed for one more precious memory to share.

"Please, don't go. I'll hurry. Stay." She rushed off to her tent to gather the one treasure she wanted to share with her grandmother.

Breathlessly, Sarah returned to the acacia tree where she had left Miriam sitting in the shade. Panic struck her as she saw her grandmother sitting quietly, almost lifeless, her head on her raised knees, her arms wrapped around her legs. Was she dead. "Oh dear, God, no!"

Her panicked exclamation awakened Miriam, causing her to laugh.

"Don't worry, darling. I'm still here. I don't think it will happen that way."

"Please, Softa, I want to be with you when He comes to get you. Can I?"

"I don't know, darling, it isn't up to me. I doubt it though. I have the sense in my spirit that I'll just leave and no one will know. I'll just leave."

"No. Please. Ask Him to let me be with you."

"Sarah. Trust. Okay? Just trust God. It will be okay whether you are with me or not. You have a family to take care of. That's enough. Now, what was it you wanted to show me?"

"This." Sarah held up a small oil lamp obviously made by a child. "Do you remember when you taught us how to do this? You taught us to look for the right clay. To mix it with water and shape it into these amazing lamps."

"Yes, I remember." Miriam reached for the lamp and all the memories it contained. "We had been going through a hard time. It wasn't long after the fire struck the edges of the camp due to the complaining of the riff raft that came with us out of Egypt. Everyone was tense, tired, cranky and scared. Parents were impatient with their children, even your ema, my sweet daughter-in-law, who was normally so patient with you, was cranky.

"I felt like I had to do something to help so I took you, your siblings and some of the other children from the Levitical tribe and we went into the foothills hunting for clay. We found a lot of it. We gathered some of it and brought it back to the encampment and I taught you how to mix it with water. After it sat for a while we worked it and then shaped it into oil lamps. I cannot believe you still have yours."

"It has always been special to me. That was the first day that I began to feel like a big girl. I know I was tiny, maybe only three, but you made me feel so big and so important. Your hands on mine shaping the lamp, making it ready to put in the fire. It was almost magic. Every time we pulled up camp, *Ema* carefully wrapped it for me in a scarf and tucked it into a bag just for me to carry. She knew how much I treasured it. Now I keep it close to my bed. I still use it. Not as much as I used to, but I do still use it. I'll use it every night now…" Sarah's voice trailed off. She didn't want to finish the thought. She didn't want to speak the words. It was too real. Too soon.

"Don't worry. You will show your own grandchildren how to make those same lamps, but it will be in the Promised

Land. You will have the joy of establishing roots in the Promised Land where you and your family will settle down, build real homes, have businesses and raise several generations before you have to leave again. It will be truly wonderful."

"Leave again? Why would we leave again after all that we've been through to get there? What do you know? What do you see?"

"Few things last forever. God's promises to us are that the Promised Land is ours forever. However, the day will come when we won't deserve it and he'll allow us to go into captivity once again where we'll stay for a very long time. When we do return to the land, it will be for the last time and it will be at a very high price. Nations will be against us. Many of our people will be sacrificed in the flames of monsters. It will be hard. But, in the end, God will bring us back and we'll stay in the land forever. Really forever."

Shocked at her grandmother's words, Sarah sat in silence. She was almost angry at her grandmother for such a terrible statement yet wisdom reminded her that her grandmother was a prophet and could see into the future that which others couldn't see. Could it be that she was right? Was it only temporary, our time in the land? Surely not.

"Don't worry, Darling. You won't see it. Your children and their children won't see it. It will happen. But when we return, the entire world will know and we will dance in the streets. The lives of that generation will bleed out on the streets but their blood will nourish the ground and fertilize the soil and we will grow."

Seventeen—The Leaving

The first light of morning spread its thin fingers through the dark goat skin tent reaching down and touching the very still body of Miriam on the couch-bed where she lay. She was gone. Just as quietly as she had entered this earth one hundred and twenty seven years before, in the land of Goshen, in the country of Egypt, she had left. She had walked a holy and righteous life, bringing laughter and joy to many. Her lifeless face bore a sweet smile leaving those left behind to wonder at what it was she saw as she followed The Light into another realm.

In the Wilderness of Zin, at Kadesh, the people mourned the loss of their beloved Miriam.

And the community was without water.

"For I do not want you to be unaware, brothers, that our Fathers were all under the cloud, and all passed through the sea, and all ate the same spiritual food, and all drank the same spiritual drink. For they drank from the spiritual rock that followed them, and the Rock was Christ."
—I Corinthians 10: 1 - 4

Glossary

Abba – dad, daddy

Aggadah – story, a telling

Cubit – an ancient measure of length, approximately equal to the length of a forearm. It was typically about 18 inches or 44 cm, though there was a long cubit of about 21 inches or 52 cm

Dohd – Uncle

Dohdah – Aunt

Ema – Mother, momma

Erv – after sunset, the beginning of the next day

Lashon Hara – To speak evil (gossip) about another

Malqata – Egyptian palace

Ohel Moed – Tabernacle

Omer – ancient Hebrew dry measure, the tenth part of an ephah.

Rauch HaKodesh – Holy spirit

Saba – grandfather

Saba Rabah – Great grandfather

Softa – grandmother

Tav – the last Hebrew letter. Symbolizes truth

Tzaddik – righteous one

Tzara'at – Skin disease much like leprosy

Wadi(s) – dry river bed that can become a rushing river in the wet season

A note from the author

Prophetess is the third book in a proposed series of six on Heroines of the Bible. Like the previous books, it is a work of fiction based on biblical fact. This story starts in Genesis 46, when the family of Jacob moves to Egypt to avoid the famine in Canaan. It continues through Exodus and Numbers, finishing in 1 Corinthians. In my research for this book I have utilized many resources including, but not limited, numerous translations of the Bible, the Saperstein Edition of Rashi's Commentary on Genesis, Exodus and Numbers, as well as the Midrash, all of which I believe have added to the telling and increased our knowledge of this amazing prophetess, a true woman of God.

Miriam, the sister of Moses and Aaron, is often overlooked in sermons and teachings other than referencing Miriam's Song and the *tzara'at* affliction she suffered when she lobbied against her brother. She was a daughter, a sister, a wife, a mother, a grandmother and, in a sense, a savior of the People of God. She was a prophetess of the One True God and a very influential leader of her people.

She was a real person faced with every day challenges, not all that different than the women of today face as they try to lead their families through life. She faced slavery and freedom and passed into the next world via the kiss of God. She deserves our awareness, our respect and our taking time to ponder her and the challenges she faced.

About the Author

Margy Pezdirtz grew up on a farm in northern Oklahoma where life was simple and somewhat cloistered, never dreaming she would travel the world and meet her soul mate in Israel. Together they built a life of business, fun, adventure and service to their Lord, which came to a screeching halt when her beloved David became suddenly ill. Since his passing, Margy has continued to serve the Lord through teaching the Word of God, traveling to Israel and encouraging others to do the same.

She speaks to groups teaching others about the significance of Judea and Samaria, biblical Israel through Christian Friends of Israeli Communities (cfoic.com) where she serves as Chairman of the Board of Directors. She is an ardent Christian Zionist.

In addition to her teaching and writing ministry, she maintains two blogs:

www.heartlandheartbeat.wordpress.com and www.rekalculating.wordpress.com.

She and David have six children, 11 grandchildren and six great grandchildren. She maintains the ministry they started together, Comforters of Israel. She has written three biblical novels, *Genesis Triangle, Valor, and Prophetess* as well as her and David's story entitled *Who Will Kill the Spiders?*

Made in the USA
Columbia, SC
29 May 2018